THE
EXECUTION

THE EXECUTION

a novel

Hugo Wilcken

HarperCollins*Publishers*

HarperCollins books may be purchased for educational, business, or sales promotional use. For information, please write: Special Markets Department, HarperCollins Publishers Inc., 10 East 53rd Street, New York, NY 10022.

First published in Great Britain in 2001 by HarperCollins Publishers.

FIRST EDITION

Designed by The Book Design Group/Matt Perry Ratto

Printed on acid-free paper

Library of Congress Cataloging-in-Publication Data
Wilcken, Hugo.
    The execution/Hugo Wilcken
        p.   cm.
    ISBN 0-06-018823-5
        I. Title.

    PS3623.I53 E94   2002
    813'.6—dc21

                                    2001042410

02 03 04 05 06 ❖/RRD 10 9 8 7 6 5 4 3 2 1

THE EXECUTION

I

CHRISTIAN'S WIFE WAS KILLED IN A CAR CRASH YESTERDAY.
Apparently her brakes failed and the car careered into a shop
front. The shop was open at the time but there were no other
victims, just her. She died from asphyxiation, the seat belt
crushed her windpipe. If she hadn't been wearing her seat belt,
she might have survived.

I wouldn't say I knew her. I'd met her twice, maybe three
times, when she'd come into the office looking for Christian.
We'd probably said no more than hello to each other. She was
around thirty-five I'd say and quite good-looking—I wondered
how she'd ended up with someone like Christian. Once, about a
year ago, Christian asked me whether I wanted to go for a drink
with him and his wife, but I had something else on so I turned
him down. The invitation surprised me, because although we've

worked in the same office for the past eighteen months, I have no particular rapport with Christian and I've never socialized with him. I was with him yesterday though, when they called about his wife.

There'd been a department meeting in the morning. The news had just come in about Jarawa's sentence and we're launching a major campaign for him. Jamie's appointed me team leader, with Christian and Joanne working under me. It's my first big campaign so it's important to me. After the meeting I got cuttings and printouts from the library and looked over them until lunchtime, making notes and thinking. Then I went with Christian to the Italian sandwich bar on the corner. It's the first time I've had lunch with him alone. I've never directly worked with him either, until now. Straightaway he told me that he was pissed off I was leading the campaign and not him. I could understand his disappointment: he's about forty and I'm only twenty-nine. Besides, West Africa is "his" area. Anyway I didn't want any trouble so I said I hoped we could work as equals on this one. I proposed we divide the responsibilities evenly, while Jo, being younger and fairly inexperienced, could look after paperwork and legwork and coordinate the volunteers. My idea was that Christian could liaise with contacts in Africa while I handled government officials and the other human rights agencies. I'd also put in a visa application for him, although it was of course unlikely to be granted. The proposal pleased him. He'd wanted to be frank about the fact that he was pissed off, he said, but he knew he could work with me.

After lunch we started to flesh out our campaign strategy in his office. We'd hardly sat down, though, when the phone rang and Christian answered. It was a very brief conversation. He put down the phone and didn't say anything. He went very white and stared at me. I said, what's up? He said, she's dead, she's been killed. I automatically assumed he meant his wife—perhaps because I knew they didn't have any children. But thinking about it now, it might just as well have been his mother, or someone completely different. I didn't exactly know what to say. He just sat there, with his bloodless face. After a while he said, so what am I going to do now? and rocked a little in his chair. Then I spoke. . . . We had some sort of conversation, which I can't remember now. He must have told me it was his wife, that she'd had a car accident, that it had taken place in Oxford, where he and his wife lived. I hadn't known they lived in Oxford. It seemed a pretty long way for Christian to commute every day.

He looked so completely helpless that I suggested I drive him down to Oxford, to the hospital. I had plenty of things to do that afternoon, and no doubt someone else in the office would have done a much better job of looking after Christian, but he'd been with me when he'd found out about his wife, so somehow it seemed like my responsibility. He sat there in complete silence, still rocking in his chair and hugging himself. So eventually I stood up and said: come on, we've got to go, you can't sit here all day. I sort of got him up and took his jacket off the hanger on the back of the door and helped him into it. He was like a zombie.

We were caught up in a snarl at Marble Arch but got onto the motorway pretty quickly after that. We didn't talk. While I'd been negotiating traffic on the way out of London the silence seemed normal, but then we were flying down the motorway and it felt like there was a void that needed to be filled. On several occasions I caught myself on the point of initiating small talk, more or less as a reflex action. But that would have been even less appropriate than the void. The car engine hummed so softly and evenly in the background that after a while I couldn't hear it anymore, and it seemed as if we were in total silence. At first I didn't feel awkward, but gradually an air of acute embarrassment invaded me. I thought of putting the radio on to break the spell, but in the end decided against it. It occurred to me that

I'd been in a bit of a daze as we'd left the office, and that I'd forgotten to say to anyone where we were going or that we wouldn't be back. I had my mobile phone with me, though, and I thought of calling, but then decided against that too. I couldn't easily tell them about Christian's wife over the phone—not as he sat there beside me, in any case.

I glanced over at Christian occasionally. He was as rigid as an Egyptian statue, hands symmetrically resting on his thighs, staring blankly at the license plate of the car ahead. He was sitting so still that he didn't seem himself. Normally, Christian squirms in his seat and wrings his hands and agitates his body, like a schoolboy or a poor sleeper. It irritates me, that habit of his.

As I drove in silence, I thought about Christian. We've worked in the same department for a year and a half but he's been at Africa Action much longer. I don't dislike him, but on the other hand I don't particularly get on with him either. Despite his age there's something of the adolescent about him. With his lank, greasy hair, dirty jeans and John Lennon spectacles he looks like a seventies student. It's as if he developed a look in his teens, then never changed it. He's got a politically naïve outlook and he probably considers himself some kind of anarchist. That doesn't stop him getting intensely involved in office politics—he thinks everyone's always slighting him but ninety percent of the time it's not true. Then again, not to do him down too much, he does have his more positive side. He's honest and friendly when he's not being paranoid, and generally you can reason with him. I suppose you could say he believes in the work as well.

Something's happened to him over the past couple of months, though, and everybody at the office has noticed it. He's become more erratic. There've been days when he hasn't turned up for work. Sometimes he looks like he's been drinking or doing drugs. He's been acting a bit weirdly with people too—

the other day I heard him shouting at Fiona, when normally he's the last person to raise his voice.

I missed the turnoff, but didn't notice for a while. Eventually I turned 'round at a junction and joined the traffic going the other way. This business of overshooting the turnoff seemed to snap Christian out of his zombie phase. He started wriggling about in his seat. Then, as we were hitting Oxford, he suddenly said, "They're going to ask me to identify the body. But I don't want to. As long as I don't identify the body, she's still alive." I didn't really know what he was on about, but replied, "Don't be stupid."

He started looking around, glancing out the window, craning his neck strangely like a cat peering out of a cat box. I also noticed that his hands were shaking quite a bit now. Just before we got to the hospital, he reached into a pocket of his suede jacket and pulled out a pack of rolling tobacco. Normally I'd have asked him if he could wait until we arrived since I don't like smoke in the car, but I let it pass. He was still peering out the window and rolled the cigarette very quickly without even looking at his hands. His hands completely stopped shaking as he rolled the cigarette, then started shaking again immediately after, so that he had trouble lighting it. It reminded me of my dead grandmother, who'd had Parkinson's but could still play the piano without fumbling a single note.

We got to the hospital. I told Christian to go into casualty while I parked the car, but he wouldn't. He just sat there, puffing away at his rolled cigarette—which kept going out, so he had to keep relighting it—and not saying a word. It annoyed me for some reason. I found a parking space, got out, and went 'round to his side to help him out. But still he wouldn't budge. Finally he whimpered, "I can't go in, I can't go in." I said, "Of course you can," and tugged at his arm. At that he started to tremble, not just his hands, but his whole body, his face too. I thought he might cry as well, and I certainly wanted to avoid that. I didn't want a scene, but on the other hand I could hardly force him into the hospital. I said, "Why don't we just have a wander 'round, just take it easy?" I'd noticed a small park in the hospital grounds, and my idea was to take a walk there. I thought it might sort of limber Christian up for the hospital.

Then I had another idea. "Listen, I've got a tiny bit of dope on me, enough for a joint. We could have a joint first, then go into the hospital after. What do you say?" I had this scrap of dope left over from the bag Stephen Pusey had given me. It'd been sitting in the glove box for the past month or so and I'd almost forgotten it was there.

We walked over to the park. It was a depressing affair with weed-ridden flower beds, gravel, visitors pushing patients around in wheelchairs. Christian was walking very slowly and I had my hand under his armpit, as if he too were a patient. It must have looked ridiculous since he's quite a bit taller than me. We sat down on the only free bench and I got out the bag and handed it to Christian. "Here, you roll it, you're probably better at it than me." I watched with fascination as Christian's twitching and trembling stopped once more during the few moments it took him to roll the joint. Then he lit up and drew heavily on it, before passing it on to me wordlessly. I took a small drag and hardly inhaled—I didn't want to let Christian smoke by himself but I did have to drive back to London. Nonetheless I could feel my muscles relax from that one half-drag. It was having an instant effect on Christian as well. The trembling didn't exactly stop, but it kind of slowed down and got less intense. I passed the joint back and he smoked the rest of it over the next few minutes, staring into the gravel and muttering "Ah well, ah well" from time to time.

He smoked the joint right down, then after a final drag he tried to throw the end onto the ground. But it stuck to his fin-

gers and he couldn't shake it off, so he rubbed his hands together
and the remaining paper and crumbs of tobacco blew away in
the wind. He said: "Damn, I burnt my finger," and he put his finger in his mouth. That occupied him for a moment and then he
looked up. I could see from his eyes that he was pretty out of it.
He was gazing at the bench opposite us, which was next to a
fountain that didn't work. On the bench sat an extremely old
woman with a blanket 'round her shoulders in spite of the warm
weather, and a middle-aged woman, probably her daughter, who
was shouting at her, "I said, Eileen and Jack are moving to Amer-
ica!" But the old woman was paying no attention whatsoever—
she was making a strange clicking sound with her teeth.
Christian turned to me and said, "Look at those two women.
The sick one's not paying a blind bit of notice to what the other
one's saying. It's pretty funny!" He started laughing and then so
did I. I said, "You're right, she couldn't give a damn!" and we
both laughed again. After we'd finished laughing, Christian put
his hand on my shoulder and said, "You're a friend. You know
that?" He seemed choked with emotion and looked again as
though he might cry. I said, "Of course. Of course I'm a friend."
He stared at me with his dilated eyes. "You know I have to tell
you something very, very important. I have to tell you. It's a terrible thing." I said, "No, you don't have to tell me anything." He
insisted, "Yes, there's something I have to tell you. It's very
important." I repeated, "No, you don't have to tell me anything."

I walked him to casualty. At the reception desk I filled in a
form for him, then a nurse, an Irish woman, showed us to a dis-
mal waiting room. I asked how long we would have to wait, she
said she didn't know. We sat there in silence for a moment, next
to each other. The seats were made of orange plastic and the
brown carpet had cigarette burns in it. I resisted the temptation
to pick up and flick through one of the dog-eared women's
magazines that lay on a smoked-glass table; it didn't seem the

right thing to do. There was a young couple in the waiting room too, but then they left and we were alone. I was wondering when it would be opportune for me to leave too. Could I go now or should I wait until Christian had seen the doctor? Or should I drive him back home after he'd seen the doctor? Should I try to get hold of one of his relatives, his wife's parents, for example, or had the hospital already done that? It was a novel situation and I didn't really know what was expected of me.

Suddenly Christian started talking. Not about his wife, and not about the "important thing" I'd stopped him telling me in the park, but about Jarawa. He said he thought this new campaign for his reprieve was a total waste of time. There was a peculiar violence to his voice and I was a little taken aback by this sudden outburst.

I said, "I don't agree, I don't agree."

He shook his head. "He's a dead man. They won't stop now. It's in the logic of things. They'll kill him like the ones before."

"No. This is different, because the others had as much blood on their hands as their executioners."

Christian was watching me intensely as I spoke. My words seemed to ignite something in him, he started getting all excited and worked up. That's not the issue, that's not the issue, he said. Didn't I see that it was no longer about saving one man or another? Didn't I see that in the long term it was immaterial whether one man died or not, that the question wasn't there, it was elsewhere? Not the death of one man . . . He ranted on for a while, stumbling over his words, but I didn't really understand what he was driving at, or perhaps I simply wasn't listening. I wondered why Jarawa's fate suddenly seemed so important to Christian, when his wife had just died. Perhaps it was the dope, or maybe it had something to do with the shock.

The nurse came out. At first Christian didn't notice, though. He'd got so involved in his tirade and was staring at me in this very intense way. Finally she interrupted to ask which one of us was Mr. Tedeschi. Christian went silent and the blood drained from his face again. He made a feeble signal with his hand, then got up and shuffled along behind the nurse. He somehow looked absurd. He looked like he'd just been called up to the headmaster's office or something. He certainly didn't look like his wife had just been killed.

I glanced up at the ugly, functional clock hanging on the wall. It was ten to three. I wondered again whether I could go now. I wondered whether from here on, the hospital would deal with Christian, call his family, take him home, etc. But then the nurse came out again and asked me whether she could have a word with me. Without waiting for a reply, she sat down in Christian's seat and leaned toward me so that her knees almost touched mine. She had very dark blue eyes that were almost black, like Marianne's. Was I a relative or perhaps a close friend of Mr. Tedeschi's, she asked me. I said I was a friend. Perhaps you'd like to know what exactly happened, she said. Then she started giving me all the details about Christian's wife's death—the failed brakes, the seat belt, and all the rest. I listened, then at one point said, "But should you be telling me all this?" She looked at me with surprise. After a moment's silence, she asked me if I knew Christian's family at all, whether he had any brothers or sisters, were his parents still alive, and if so did I know how to get in contact with them, because "what Mr. Tedeschi will need now is a lot of support from his family." I told her I knew absolutely nothing about Christian's family, only that he had no children. I see, she said, and looked at me sourly. I said I was sorry I couldn't help her but she continued to frown. She was acting as if she'd been flirting with me and I'd rebuffed her or something. I almost felt like saying, "It wasn't me who killed his wife." Finally she said thank you, then got up and left.

I waited. Through the ventilators I could hear a doctor murmuring, "It shouldn't hurt," and the reply, "It hurts, Jesus!" I picked up a magazine and flicked through it, then started reading an article about wartime experiments on concentration camp detainees. There were photos as well. It was quite interesting, but finally it repelled me and I put the magazine down. I was tired. I even started to doze a little but then I heard shouts. It sounded like Christian's voice. I heard a woman trying to remonstrate with him, but he cut her off with more shouts. A door opened somewhere. I heard the woman say, "Mr. Tedeschi, Mr. Tedeschi!" Christian was shouting, "I won't let you do it to me. Why do you want to do it to me?" After that there were footsteps, and the intermingled voices of two men, "No one's going to make you do anything. No one's going to make you do anything." A door shut, then opened, then more footsteps, then silence.

A woman with an open white coat appeared in the waiting room. She looked to be in her mid-thirties and had prematurely gray hair, which she made no effort to hide. Her face wore a vaguely troubled expression. Looking my way, she asked, "Are you Mr. Tedeschi's friend?" I replied that I wasn't exactly his friend, more his colleague. She appeared to think for a moment, then asked me to come into her office.

I followed her down a corridor, then into a windowless, airless room. As I sat down, she began to speak in those modulated, "reasonable" tones that only priests and doctors use. The problem, she said, is that Mr. Tedeschi is extremely upset, naturally, and he's not acting very rationally. We've given him a sedative and he's lying down at the moment. . . . What we really need to do is inform his wife's relatives. . . . Unfortunately, Mr. Tedeschi was too upset to help us. I said, "I'm afraid I'm going to disappoint you as well, since I don't know any of his wife's relatives." I added that I didn't even know if her parents were dead or alive. "I see, I see," the woman said. She seemed to ignore me for a moment and I wondered whether the interview was over. All of a sudden she continued, "But you did know Susan Tedeschi?" I said I'd met her on two or three occasions, yes. She got out something from a desk drawer and handed it to me. It was an international driving license, in the name of Susan Tedeschi. I looked at the murky photograph. It certainly looked like Christian's wife—a much younger version of her—but then again I don't know if I'd have recognized it as her if her name hadn't been on the license. The doctor asked, "Is that her?" I replied that I thought it was, adding that the driving license was in her name, at any rate.

The doctor then introduced herself, which seemed odd because normally you either introduce yourself at the beginning of an encounter or not at all. After we'd exchanged names, she started talking about Christian's wife again. She spoke very slowly, as if to a child or a foreigner. She said the problem was that as Mr. Tedeschi was "incapacitated" for the moment, they really needed someone to identify the body. Since Mrs. Tedeschi's maiden name was Smith, it was going to take a while to track down her family. Would I perhaps be prepared to "step in"? Before I had the chance to respond, she quickly added, "Perhaps I can get you a cup of coffee?" I replied, "No, I never drink coffee in the afternoon."

There was an uncomfortable pause. I was starting to feel a little sticky on account of the heat and the stuffiness of the room. I was also wondering whether I should tell the doctor that Christian had already had a joint before they'd given him the sedative. But in the end I said nothing. The doctor continued, "It would only take a minute or two. We can go right now if you like, and get it over and done with immediately." I couldn't think of a reply so I remained silent. I didn't particularly want to identify the body, nor could I think of any reason why I shouldn't. The doctor sensed my hesitancy. "I saw her myself when she came in. I can fully assure you she looks perfectly all right. You'll just have to see her face for a couple of seconds, that's all. Her

eyes will be closed. She sustained no head injuries whatsoever."
Then she stood up and said, "Really, we'll get it over and done
with right now, then you won't have to worry about it anymore," and she started moving toward the door.

We went down a lift and got out somewhere below ground
level. We were in a harshly lit corridor with no natural light at
all. As we walked, I wondered whether morgues were always
underground. If so, perhaps it was because it had been a means of
keeping bodies cold, before the invention of refrigeration I
mean. Or perhaps it was for a more metaphorical reason. In any
case, it was a stupid thing to waste time thinking about, since I
didn't even know if morgues were always underground. The
woman led me through more corridors. There seemed to be a
maze of them and I quickly lost my sense of direction. Electrical
wiring and water pipes hung down from the low, dusty ceiling.
At one point, I said, "But really, I only knew her very slightly.
Perhaps I won't even recognize her." I really thought I might
not. "That's no problem," answered the doctor, "all you say then
is that you don't recognize her, and that's the end of it." I said,
"Then what's the point?"—but we'd already arrived at the
room.

She was lying on a trolley, with two white sheets draped over
her. There was a morgue assistant there, a young guy with tied-
back hair and a goatee beard, perhaps a student. We'd interrupted
a game of solitaire he'd been playing at a desk on the far side of
the room. He wheeled the body over to us, then removed the
sheets from her face with great delicacy, as if he were a beauti-
cian about to give someone a facial. I stared. I'd never actually
seen a dead body before. Alex once told me he'd been so anxious
the first time he was confronted with a corpse in anatomy class
that he'd gone to the toilet afterward and thrown up. Staring at
the face, I didn't feel anything in particular. A long, faint scratch

mark crossed her high forehead diagonally from left to right, like a line drawn across a page to strike it out.

It was her all right. It was Susan Tedeschi. Or perhaps she called herself Susan Smith. I hadn't even remembered that her first name was Susan until the doctor reminded me. And I'd thought I might not recognize her face, but I did. It transfixed me momentarily. I probably only looked for a few seconds, but it seemed much longer. They must have hosed down the body or something because her hair was all wet and combed back. It made her look more lifelike, as if she'd only just this minute stepped out of the shower. In other ways too she appeared much as she'd been in life, but there were subtle differences. Her skin was gray rather than pink, although that might also have been the effect of the fluorescent lights, which seemed to drain the color out of everything else in the morgue. Another difference was the expression on her face. On the two or three occasions I'd seen her previously, she'd seemed quite meek. About the only thing Christian had ever told me about his wife was that once he'd arranged to meet her at a party, but she'd never turned up. Then on leaving, he'd spotted their car in the street opposite the house where the party was being held, with his wife sitting inside. Apparently she'd had some kind of panic attack.

In death, though, she looked anything but meek. Her face wore a stern, implacable expression and she seemed almost powerful.

I turned to the doctor. "Yes, that's her." She seemed visibly relieved. The morgue assistant flicked the two sheets perfectly back into place in one smooth action, which reminded me of Christian's skill in rolling cigarettes. Then he wheeled the body away.

"Wait here a moment please," the doctor said. "I'll be back in a second." She disappeared and I was left alone with the morgue assistant. He stood around uneasily, obviously not wanting to go back to his game of solitaire while I was still in the room. It was difficult to know what kind of small talk to make to a morgue assistant, though.

"So what happens now? To the body I mean."

"Umm, they'll probably do an autopsy."

"Really? How do they decide that? I mean, how do they decide which bodies they're going to do an autopsy on?"

"Well there's all these categories. I can't remember offhand. Accidents, suicides, deaths in custody—"

"That's interesting. I mean I never thought about what happens to the bodies. It's strange."

I waved my hand vaguely to encompass the morgue, the morgue assistant and the enormous fridges with metal doors like prison cells.

"Well it's pretty weird at first, yeah. But then you get used to it."

I thought he'd stopped and I was about to say something else when he abruptly continued, "It's the babies that are the hardest. They haven't been given a chance. You're holding it in your arms, you know it's dead but you can't resist the impulse to support its head, not to let it drop back."

I stared at him, momentarily lost for words. Just then the doctor appeared at the door. Sorry to leave you waiting like that, she said, without explaining where she'd been or what she'd been up to. She hustled me out of the morgue and we made our way back through the maze of corridors to the lift. Upstairs, I had to sign a declaration and then I was free to go. What with Christian under sedation, there didn't seem to be any point in hanging around any longer.

I made it back to London in fifty minutes. At first I thought I'd go straight home, then I changed my mind and went into the West End and parked the car in the underground car park at work. I thought I might find Jo and get going on the Jarawa campaign; we could at least rough out an initial press release for the London papers. But as I waited for the lift, it occurred to me that if I went into the office I'd have to talk about Christian and I didn't want to do that. So I left the car park on foot by the car exit and started to walk aimlessly toward Covent Garden. I wasn't really thinking about Christian. But his wife's face was still in front of me, in a way, with its single scratch on the forehead. Eventually I decided to go for a swim. The private swimming pool where I'm a member was five minutes' walk away, just off Shaftesbury Avenue.

It was an odd pleasure to open my locker and see my swimming and shower gear there, just as I'd left it last time. I changed quickly: I wanted to get into the pool as fast as possible. It was still only five-fifteen, which meant that there was hardly anyone around yet—the pool doesn't usually fill up until six or six-thirty, when people start knocking off work. There was one old man who was swimming extremely slowly, doing one lap to my three or four. He was very hairy, his body and prominent breasts were covered in fine silver hair like some aquatic animal, and it seemed a big struggle for him to keep his head above water. Finally he got out—taking ages to climb up the little ladder— and collapsed breathlessly onto a poolside bench. The afternoon light splashed in through the skylights overhead.

I felt much better after my swim. I felt cleansed. I looked at myself in the mirror and felt reassured by the healthy young man staring back at me. In the changing room I bumped into Phil. He was looking for someone to play a few games of squash with, but I told him I'd just swum fifteen hundred meters and was feeling pretty whacked.

I walked back to the car park and picked up the car. As I drove, I noticed for the first time since the morning what a beautiful day it was, or had been. Soft blue sky, Dutch wisps of cloud, a hazy warmth. It felt more like July than May. I opened up the sunroof, partly to let the sun stream in, partly to rid the car of the smell from Christian's cigarette. An old Golf convertible stood beside me at the lights, pumping out music. The three young guys inside were wearing sunglasses and had taken their shirts off. The driver looked my way and grinned. I slammed my foot down on the accelerator when the lights changed but the Golf was too quick. As the car sped off, the driver honked his horn at me and I honked back.

I passed by an art gallery in Mayfair and suddenly remembered Marianne's opening at Joseph Kimberly. She'd been nervous about it all week. But I'd completely forgotten—this whole business with Christian's wife had driven it from my mind. Now it occurred to me that there was no point in going back to Camberwell if I had to be at Primrose Hill by half-past seven. As I passed Hyde Park I noticed a parking spot and pulled up without thinking about it too much. I just wanted to make the most of the vestiges of the warm afternoon. So I got out and wandered around on the south side of the park for a while near Rotten Row then sat down under a tree. Despite the hot weather, the grass still had that Astroturf sheen the spring rain had given it. It looked unripe, is what Marianne might have said.

There were quite a few people around, for a Monday evening. Rollerbladers crisscrossed the paths. A black guy came 'round selling drinks on ice. I bought a can of beer from him and knocked it back quickly. Then I moved out of the shade and lay down, with my eyes shut, to feel the warmth of the sun on my face. I could hear a riot of evening birdsong, the good-humored shouts of guys playing football, and the hum of traffic. The grass was prickly and smelled sweet.

It was about then that I first felt a surging sense of well-being, or perhaps contentment. It mystified me at first but what it was, it soon struck me, was that Christian's wife had left me. She'd accompanied me all the way from Oxford but my long swim had slowly washed her all away. I was back to how I had been before the events of the day, only more so. I felt the grass under me and the sun above me and it seemed to me that I was exactly where I wanted to be in my life. I was with the woman I wanted to be with, doing what I wanted to do. There was the Jarawa campaign, which presented itself to me like a puzzle to be solved.

I thought about my first day at Africa Action, eighteen months ago. Oliver, the guy I was replacing, had spent the afternoon showing me the ropes and had taken me out for a drink after work. We'd discussed his last campaign—it was for a Syrian dissident who'd been sentenced to death for treason. Oliver had arranged a last-minute meeting with Syrian and European Union officials to secure the guy's release. I remembered him saying to me, "It's a strange feeling when you've played a part in saving someone's life. Almost like you've saved your own."

I felt angry with Christian for saying that the Jarawa campaign was a waste of time. I felt angry that he'd said this to me after his wife's death, and not before, during the morning's department meeting. But in any case, he was quite wrong about it. He was wrong about many things. The pieces seemed to slot into place. I would save Jarawa's life, I decided. His existence would depend on me. Of course I was making wild claims for myself, but it was the way I felt momentarily, like a minor god.

The sun was setting and I dragged myself to my feet, a little drugged with this feeling that was washing through and out of me.

II

THE GALLERY WAS ALREADY STARTING TO FILL UP AS I GOT THERE. Marianne had brought Jessica along as well, because Jane's away and Marianne's fussy about other baby-sitters. Jessica was in an unmanageable state of excitement and was shouting and pulling at the dresses and trouser legs of the people who'd already arrived. She's going through a really hyperactive phase at the moment. I was wondering what to do with her when all of a sudden she sat down, curled up, and went straight to sleep in the middle of the gallery space, right under everyone's feet. I tried to wake her up and get her to come with me but she wouldn't—you can't wake a child that wants to sleep. But she couldn't stay there so I picked her up, took her into the office, and laid her down on the couch. She curled up again then started snoring, very gently. I sat down beside her for a moment and put my arm across her. Messily stacked up against the office walls were paintings, twenty or thirty of them. Opposite the couch was an enormous piece of slate that must have weighed a ton. On it had been painted a picture of a naked woman, in a primitive style. She was asleep on the ground.

I went back into the gallery and had a beer, then another. After an hour or so the place started to get pretty crowded and it was getting difficult to move around. I lost track of Marianne, and for a while I just stood in a corner and watched the other people. Broadly speaking they divided into two categories. There were older, conservatively elegant white couples or single men, who stood around talking in slightly tired voices, drinking white wine and generally not smoking. Then there was a younger crowd in their twenties who drank beer and smoked and were louder. Some of these were artists, some were students, others were friends of Marianne, and a few were all three. I knew only one or two of them—I keep clear of that side of Marianne's life—but they all seemed to know each other. Fragments of conversation strayed my way . . . to my left, a couple discussed a mutual acquaintance, dumped by her husband for a younger woman. She was in hospital now after a last-ditch face-lift gone wrong. To my right, I heard someone remark of one of Marianne's larger works, "There's something very extreme about it." I glanced over to the painting in question. It was very colorful. I couldn't see what was extreme about it but I wondered nonetheless if the person had a point. It's not something Marianne and I ever talk about.

A woman in her early thirties came up to me. "Remember me?" I said no, I'm sorry I don't. "You don't remember a big argument about South Africa at a dinner party? Ages ago, at Nick Tate's place." Then I remembered. Her name's Charlotte Fisher. She's South African and she used to go out with Nick. She's quite pushy and good-looking in an American sitcom kind of way. I remembered the dinner party—it was a long time ago, maybe even before Marianne. She'd taken violent exception to some comment of mine. She'd launched into a great polemic about how her mother's maid back in Johannesburg was like part of the family and if she wasn't working for them she'd be on the streets and her children wouldn't have enough to eat. And how could I possibly know what it's like when I'd never been to South Africa, how did I dare comment?

I didn't particularly want to talk to her but since it didn't look like I had an option I asked her what she was up to nowadays. She said she'd gone back to South Africa for a while, but had recently come back to set up her own PR business, promoting artists. She dropped a few names of artists she'd recently signed up, including one I'd vaguely heard of, a German woman who's been getting a lot of publicity lately for her blown-up photos of dead people. I said I thought the photos were pretty sensationalist. That's more or less the point, replied Charlotte. We chatted and jousted about that for a while. I looked around for Marianne, but she seemed to be involved in a very earnest conversation with a middle-aged man. So Charlotte and I continued drinking and talking. She asked me how I met Marianne and I told her about the beach in Portugal. Then she asked me about Marianne's work. French artists are very in vogue at the moment, she said. She seemed very interested in Marianne.

I asked if she was still with Nick. She laughed sourly. "God no, we split up a couple of years ago." She didn't seem embarrassed I'd asked though, just as she hadn't been embarrassed that I'd initially forgotten who she was. Then she recounted the story of her breakup—telling it as if it were a funny joke, with climaxes, anticlimaxes, and a punch line. She'd gone home late one evening, when Nick thought she was out of town, and she'd literally found him in bed with another woman. She immediately moved out—it was Nick's house after all. She thought she'd get over the relationship quickly but found herself doing obsessive

things like taking time off work to spy on Nick. To make matters
worse, the other woman had moved straight in with Nick. So
she decided that what she really wanted was revenge. But it had
to be the right kind, "Nasty, but not too nasty." Eventually she
hit upon the solution. One day she happened on a newspaper
article about a private detective who used call girls to entrap
wayward husbands. So she went to see him, posing as a worried
wife, and ended up paying him a lot of money to get a call girl
to entice Nick up to a hotel room. The whole encounter was
captured on video, which she then sent to Nick's new girlfriend.
Later she'd found out through a mutual friend that the couple
had split up not long after.

"And you didn't feel guilty about it afterward?"

"Well, he might have lost his girlfriend, but at least I gave
him a good time!"

I laughed for quite a while. We laughed together. I was reasonably drunk by this stage. There were a lot of people in the gallery
and we had to stand very close to each other with our shoulders
almost touching. I wondered whether the story Charlotte had just
told me was true or whether it was a sort of party piece. In the end
I decided it didn't matter much. She was wearing a black dress
made of a light gauze-like material, and I noticed that her breasts
were almost visible beneath it. As I looked up from her décolleté I
caught her eyes. She smiled at me and said nothing.

We continued talking for another ten minutes and then
finally she spotted someone else she knew and drifted off. I
thought of catching up with Marianne and looked about for
her, but she was still talking to the middle-aged man. I watched
them for a moment. The man seemed somehow out of place at a
gallery opening. He looked more earnest than elegant. He and
Marianne seemed to be staring at each other quite intensely as
they spoke, and at one moment I thought I saw the man's hand
slip down and gently brush Marianne's buttocks. I might have

been wrong, of course, or maybe in the crush his hand had been pushed that way. It annoyed me anyway.

Then at some point, fairly late on in the evening I think, when quite a few people had already left, Jessica came out. She looked terrified. I supposed that she'd simply woken up disoriented, not recognizing where she was, and that's what had frightened her. She ran up to me immediately, which was strange, because normally if anything's the matter she goes straight to Marianne and not me. Anyway she hugged my legs and I picked her up and asked her what was wrong.

"Daddy, there's a dead lady in the other room."

"Don't be silly, of course there isn't!"

But she just kept on repeating, "Yes there is, there's a dead lady in the other room."

Eventually I said, "Well, let's go and have a look then," but she buried her head in my shoulder and started to whimper. Just then I spotted Marianne: she was talking to somebody else now and her eyes were sort of glazed over, which meant she was drunk and happy. I offloaded Jessica onto her because I wanted to go and have a look in the office. What I thought might have happened was that perhaps some woman had drunk too much and had crawled off to the office and fallen asleep on the floor.

But there was no one in the office. Jessica must have been making it all up after all. She makes things up sometimes, as a way of attracting attention. Kids do. Nonetheless, something about this "dead lady" business disturbed me, and I sat down on the couch for a few minutes. That was when I noticed the huge slate slab again, with the picture of the sleeping woman painted on it. It must have been what frightened her. I felt momentarily relieved, but still perplexed.

It had seemed a little odd to hear Jessica say the word "dead." In fact I'd never heard her say it before. I wondered what exactly she'd meant by it. Maybe she meant the same as sleeping. Then again, that didn't seem to be the case, because she'd seen Marianne asleep often enough, and that didn't scare her. I sat on the couch for about ten minutes, thinking about that. Then my mind switched to Jarawa and the campaign: there was his appeal to plan and I started thinking through the details. We needed someone else to liaise with people on the ground, now that Christian was out of action.

For some reason I'd closed the door to the office. Now it opened. It was Charlotte, the South African woman. She'd been looking for me to say good-bye. "Well here I am," I said, and got up off the couch. She was quite red-faced. She said she was glad to have bumped into me again and maybe we could have lunch sometime—maybe she, Marianne, and I could all get together. I said I'd like that and got out one of the cards I'd just had printed up, while she rummaged about in her handbag for one of hers. I leaned down to kiss her good-bye, because she's quite a bit shorter than me. Then I put my hand 'round her waist and she put hers under my shirt and we started kissing again. We stayed like that for a moment, then we sort of collapsed onto the couch and she slipped her arms out of her dress and we continued to kiss. She was stretched out on top of me. I could feel her breathing and trembling. The rumbling noise from the gallery came and went in waves, punctuated by bursts of laughter. The door was open now and there was a real danger of someone coming in— in a way that merely heightened the sense of pleasure. I hooked my arms 'round her, but she seemed to be in her own world and quite unaware of anything, almost unaware of me as well.

Then at one point I heard a male voice, I don't know whose, and it seemed almost next to me, quite separate from the indistinct hum of conversation from beyond the door. It was enough to snap me out of my mesmeric state. I sat up abruptly, put one hand over Charlotte's mouth, the other over her breasts—I don't know why—and looked around. But there was no one there; the voice must have been some kind of acoustic trick. Charlotte smiled at me and started kissing me again. She wanted to have sex right there in the office, but I said no, we couldn't. I said I'd give her a ring tomorrow though, if she wanted, and she nodded as I helped her put her bra and dress back on. She got a little mirror out of her bag and mouthed, "Oh God." It was true her makeup was a bit of a mess now. Instead of fixing it up though, she just wiped it all off with a tissue. Then she wiped the lipstick off my lips and cheeks with another tissue and that felt intimate, more so than our kisses. She reapplied her lipstick, combed her hair back into place, and asked me, "Do I look all right?" I said she looked great. I meant it, because she'd been wearing too much makeup before and somehow looked more real now. She looked quite a bit like Susan Tedeschi, it occurred to me. Physically they're the same type, in any case. They have the same long, streaky blond hair, the same high forehead, and they're the same height. This disturbed me for a moment or two, but I dismissed it easily enough.

Charlotte left. I went out into the gallery about five minutes later. The crowd of people had thinned out considerably. I looked about for Jessica. She'd climbed out of Marianne's arms and had captured the attention of a young woman in a smart emerald dress. The woman had crouched down to her level, and Jessica was carefully explaining something to her. Then the woman laughed, and Jessica giggled as well. The strange terror had gone from her face.

We ended up taking a cab home around eleven, since we were both too drunk to drive—although I might have driven anyway, if we hadn't had Jessica with us. Marianne was flushed with excitement, because the evening had gone really well and she'd sold nine paintings, which is the most she's ever sold. In the cab, I surprised myself by saying, "Who was that guy you were talking to? The middle-aged-looking guy. You talked to him for ages." I hadn't realized I was so annoyed by that. "Oh him," she said, "I think he's a don or a professor or something. He's just moved to London." I said, "He certainly seemed very interested in you. I saw him rub against you in a pretty indiscreet way." Marianne replied, "Really? I don't think so. He's more the gentleman type." I couldn't think of anything else to say on the matter, so I let it drop. Marianne hadn't seemed to notice my annoyance; her exuberance bubbled over into a stream of talk and gossip.

We got home and while I was putting Jessica to bed, Marianne poured herself a glass of wine, although she was pretty drunk already. She got some cheese and salad stuff out of the fridge for us as well, because we hadn't had dinner but it was too late to cook now. Then, when we'd finished eating, she took off all her clothes and started wandering about the house with her glass of wine, vaguely tidying up, reading bits of newspaper or letters that were lying about, readying herself for bed, taking makeup off, humming, all at the same time. She quite often goes through this routine when she's drunk. I watched her as she wandered about. I found her beautiful and told her so. She smiled with pleasure and went into the bedroom, while I turned on the TV and watched mindless pop videos. I could hear Jessica talking in her sleep, but she seemed quite calm, for a change—lately she's been assailed by a dream monster most nights. Then finally I went to bed. Marianne was awake and started massaging my back. She was still drunk and excited by the evening's success and wanted to make love. But I didn't feel like it for some reason. Jarawa and Jessica's dead lady kept wandering in and out of my thoughts, which were gradually, seamlessly metamorphosing into dreams.

Then just before I definitively drifted off to sleep, Marianne said something. It sounded important but I didn't hear what it was, so with a tremendous effort I turned 'round and asked her. She said, "I'm pregnant again." I said I was glad and put my arm 'round her. I could smell the wine on her breath. We haven't been trying to have another child; we've been using condoms.

But I'm pretty sure I know when she conceived. There was one time not so long ago when we were making love and the condom broke. It's happened once or twice before and I've always stopped and put another one on. But this one time I didn't—I don't know why. Anyway, Marianne said she'd had a blood test last week and then on Thursday she'd found out she was pregnant. I asked her why she hadn't told me then. She said she'd wanted to wait until after the opening. I couldn't see what that had to do with anything, but it didn't really matter.

III

I SPENT AN HOUR OR TWO IN THE LIBRARY YESTERDAY MORNING, going through the Jarawa clippings. At the same time I was making notes on my laptop, organizing details from the news articles into a life story—almost as if I were writing an obituary. After I'd finished, I looked through what I'd written. His childhood, the Sorbonne scholarship, the volumes of poetry, the 1968 events, the political career, the UN posting, the business empire . . . a feeling of boredom set in as I scrolled down. Then after a while I realized it wasn't so much boredom but frustration.

I looked at the exploded image of my face reflected in the cellophane cover of a book the librarian had got out for me. It was a compilation of profiles of African writers, published by some Canadian university. I turned to the interview with Jarawa, largely a self-serving mix of anecdotes about his early struggles. They struck a more personal note than anything in the newspaper clippings, though. There was even an apocryphal-sounding nativity story—his birth had been a difficult one and his father had supposedly remarked to the midwife, "If it's a choice between the mother and child, save the mother." That was what a malevolent uncle had told Jarawa when he was five or six. It had marked him for life and had underpinned his determination to succeed, he said.

Another of these anecdotes caught my eye. It was about a poem Jarawa had written in the sixties. The subject is a kid with Down's syndrome. He'd lived in the village where Jarawa had grown up. He wasn't allowed to come out of the house. So his whole world was the house to the garden wall. Years later Jarawa returned to his native village for a visit, and he happened to see this kid. Jarawa had grown from a child to an adult, but the kid still looked exactly the same. Jarawa had traveled around Europe and yet this kid's world was still the same house and garden.

This story reminded me of something, but I couldn't put my finger on what it was. As I photocopied the pages I wondered for the first time whether I would ever get to meet Jarawa.

When I got back to my office I checked my voice mail. There was a long, garbled message from Christian—he didn't say who he was but I recognized the slightly whining quality of his voice immediately. He sounded distraught and repeated several times that he had to talk to me about something, that it was urgent. After that there was a pause of about a minute or so and I could hear him breathing unevenly into the receiver. Finally he said he'd never forget what I'd done for him the day his wife died and then hung up. I'd been meaning to ring Christian to see how he was, but what with all the work on the Jarawa campaign I hadn't got 'round to it. He's on compassionate leave and no one's replacing him so the Jarawa team's just me, Jo and a few volunteers. I have to admit that I prefer it that way because to be frank I hadn't been looking forward to working with Christian.

I listened to the message again. I knew I should ring him back now but somehow I just didn't feel in the mood for it. So I called Marianne instead to see if she wanted to meet for lunch, but she wasn't at the gallery. She wasn't at home either. Then, flipping idly through my Filofax, I noticed the card Charlotte Fisher had given me at the gallery. I'd forgotten about her. I'd forgotten that I'd said I'd call. The phone rang for ages and just as I was about to hang up she finally answered. "Oh hi it's you—I didn't think I'd hear from you again."

"Why not? I said I'd call."

We small-talked our way cautiously around each other then finally she said she was going home to cook some pasta, why didn't I come 'round? I replied, "It's such a nice day, though, why don't we go for a picnic instead?" It's true that it was a nice day, but I also wanted to be on neutral ground—I wasn't yet sure what exactly I wanted from Charlotte.

Outside it was warm, peculiarly warm for London for this time of the year. A lot of pubs and cafés had put chairs on the pavement, dance music blared out from the open doors of clothes shops and hairdressers. People were hanging about on street corners, talking and flirting—everyone was dressed for summer and there was a sort of sexual buzz in the air. As I walked up Camden High Street to Charlotte's flat that curious sense of well-being began to surge through me again. It was like a feeling of infinite possibilities, maybe even immortality.

Charlotte had had her hair cut into a summery-looking bob and was wearing an orange cotton dress that really showed off her legs, which were lightly tanned. I'd forgotten how good-looking she was and complimented her on her appearance. I kept looking at her as we walked down the street—I could see she was getting a lot of pleasure out of my reaction to her and I knew she was still interested in me.

We bought some picnic stuff from Safeway and went to Regent's Park. For a while we ate in silence, watching the joggers—middle-aged men with tortured faces—and the mothers and au pairs with their babies. Then after a few minutes Charlotte put me through a kind of interrogation. First she wanted to know how many times I'd been unfaithful to Marianne. Only once, I replied, a few years ago, before Jessica was born. As I said the word "born," I remembered how Marianne had told me the other day that she was pregnant again. I've been so busy that we've barely talked about it since and it hasn't really sunk in—it struck me now that having a second child would in some ways mean an even more radical change than having the first: a couple with a child is still a couple with a child, but two children means a proper family.

Charlotte asked me lots of questions about my infidelity. But it was so long ago and had been so brief that I could hardly remember anything about it. She was Australian; she'd had that Australian habit of ending sentences on a rising note. She was about nineteen or twenty and on her year out from college, doing a stint in London at Bryant Allen. We'd slept together a few times in her cramped South Kensington bedsit, which she shared with another Australian girl, who would be sent to stay on a friend's floor while I was there.

Charlotte wanted to know whether Marianne had ever found out about the "affair." I said I didn't think so. She asked if I thought Marianne would have left me if she'd found out and I answered, "How would I know?" But didn't you feel guilty, she pursued. I said no. Why not, she asked, didn't I have any obligations toward Marianne, didn't I want to make her happy?

I thought about that for a moment. Finally I answered that yes, certainly I have obligations, certainly I want to make Marianne happy, and that means that if I'm unfaithful I should keep it separate from our life together.

"In other words, if you lie about it, it's all right."

Again I thought.

"No, because if she ever confronted me outright, I'd tell her the truth."

She was about to interrupt me but I wanted to pursue my line of reasoning. I told her it was more subtle than that. Marianne essentially knows who I am, she probably realizes I'm capable of infidelity, but in the end she doesn't want to know the details, because as long as it's an abstract and not a concrete reality, she doesn't really care one way or the other. Charlotte said she didn't believe that. She said she didn't believe there was a woman in the world who didn't care one way or the other. And she said she didn't believe either that deep down everyone knows what their partners are really like. She, for one, had never suspected that Nick was being unfaithful.

I didn't answer her. Then after a pause she said she didn't quite know what to make of me, but I was probably some kind of bastard. She said it half-jokingly, half-seriously. We both laughed and after that we didn't talk anymore. We looked at each other quite intensely and I noticed that her eyes were purple-blue, like a bruise. We kissed. The lunch had made me drowsy and I lay down on the grass. The sun slid behind a streak of clouds, but it was still warm. . . . I stared up into the sky and thought I could make out the shadow of the moon, then I closed my eyes. Charlotte was resting her head against my chest. The weight of it had the effect of making me aware of my own breathing. I felt the air enter my lungs. I put my arm 'round Charlotte and could feel her chest rise up and down as well. I was so relaxed and it felt so good to have Charlotte's head against my chest that for a bizarre moment I felt I almost loved her.

I walked Charlotte back to her flat, and while we walked she asked me a lot of questions about Marianne and her painting. She wanted to know how she was represented and did I think she might be interested in signing up for a better financial package. The trouble with a lot of the more thoughtful artists, she said, was that they were so show orientated they tended to miss "the bigger picture." They didn't understand the need to "cultivate themselves more generally in the media." I said I didn't know, but Marianne seemed quite happy with Joseph Kimberly. He's a charming man, of course, but totally incompetent, said Charlotte.

Outside her door we kissed for a while, clumsily. Eventually Charlotte asked me in and got a bottle of champagne out of the fridge. We didn't drink it though, because we started kissing again then went to the bedroom and undressed each other. We lay down on the bed and Charlotte ran her fingers across my shoulders. Your body's so nice and taut, she said, how do you keep it like that? I stay in shape, I said, I swim, I play squash. The curtains were drawn and the room was dark like some seedy boudoir. For a long time we made love in silence, then at some point I said wait a second, I've got a condom. But Charlotte said no, let's not bother with that.

Afterward we dozed for half an hour then Charlotte got up and went into the sitting room. I could hear her speaking to someone on the phone but couldn't make out what she was saying. The tone sounded intimate though. I heard her go into the bathroom and I opened my eyes and looked around the room. It was a mess of clothes and open drawers, with various pots, lotions and lipsticks lying on every available surface. It was the exact opposite of our bedroom back at home—Marianne has a mania for tidiness. In amongst the heap of clothes on the floor I noticed a discarded pair of men's underpants that were not my own. It annoyed me. Not because Charlotte had a lover, but because she couldn't be bothered to take the most elementary steps to hide the fact.

Charlotte came back with two glasses of champagne but I didn't really feel like drinking. I watched her with curiosity as she walked about, sipped the champagne, brushed her hair out of her eyes with her hand. The way she did these things was so different to Marianne. Charlotte said, Why are you looking at me like that? Like what, I asked. Like your eyes are following my every movement. I said I like the way you move. Well don't look at me like that, she replied, it makes me feel self-conscious. It gives me the creeps. Okay, I murmured, and I closed my eyes. I could feel her getting back into bed and we made love again, then dozed a little more in each other's arms. Eventually I got up though. I had to get back to work.

I bought the *Guardian* to read on the tube as I traveled back into the West End. They'd put Jarawa on the bottom of the front page. The headline read African Writer and Diplomat Receives Death Sentence. Inside, there was more coverage and a potted biography as well, with the usual stuff about his political career and the books he'd written. A right-wing Cambridge professor was quoted as saying he considered Jarawa's poetry "dreadful doggerel," rated only because of the color of the author's skin.

A photo of Jarawa accompanied the article. I'd already seen it that morning, while going through the clippings. It must be over thirty years old, taken when he was a student in France. He looks quite striking with his extremely dark skin and fine bone structure, like a Nubian. He's posed very stiffly and he's wearing a three-piece suit that makes him look more like a thirties poet than a sixties student. There's an intense expression on his face. It's as if he were furious about something. I also noticed a watch chain dangling from his waistcoat pocket—a dandyish touch that sat strangely with his fearsome face.

When I'd left for lunch it had been strangely quiet at work; now it was bustling with people. I went back to my office and wrote out the protest letter for the ambassador, the one all the academics are signing. As I was picking up a copy from the printer to fax to the signatories for approval, I bumped into Jo and congratulated her on the *Guardian* spread. She sort of grunted in reply and refused to meet my eyes. I said, "What's up with you?" but she just walked off. I followed her down the corridor and caught up with her, "Listen, if I've done something to offend you we may as well have it out now rather than later."

"Well where the hell do you think everyone was this morning?"

"I wouldn't have a clue."

"You should have."

Then it occurred to me. It was Susan Tedeschi's funeral that morning. Jamie had sent 'round a memo with the time and place of the funeral. He'd written that he hoped everyone who'd worked with Christian would come and show solidarity at this tragic moment of his life. I'd meant to write down the details in my diary but I'd been talking to someone on the phone when whoever it was had passed me the memo, and I'd glanced over it, then put it down and continued with my conversation. After that it must have got lost in a pile of papers or something and I'd just forgotten about it. I felt bad about it but it didn't entirely account for Jo's anger. She and Christian are friends of a sort, but then so are Jo and I, and I've never had much to do with Christian.

"That's terrible of me. I'm sorry."

"It's not me you should be apologizing to, it's Christian."

Christian had apparently asked after me and had wanted to see me. I remembered the strange message on the voice mail. I told Jo I'd write him a letter, and ring him too. In a way it didn't matter. But Jo can be touchy and it's important for us not to fall out. What I mean is, it's important for the Jarawa campaign.

IV

I WAS IN MY CAR, ON THE WAY TO A MEETING IN A PARK LANE HOTEL. As I rounded Marble Arch the traffic slowly ground to a halt. It was hot; I wound down the window and gazed out at the arch. The air shimmered with the heat rising off the cars, like trees trembling in the breeze. I was thinking about the last time I'd been caught up at this same spot, a week ago, with Christian beside me—silent and stiff as he stared ahead in some kind of trance. I recalled reading somewhere that Marble Arch was where people used to be hanged, back in the seventeenth or eighteenth century.

A hotel porter showed me to a top-floor suite with sweeping views over Hyde Park. Three black guys were sitting around a conference table. Two of them were dressed in identical black suits, as if they'd just come back from a funeral. They were members of Renouveau National, Jarawa's party. They fled the country at the time of Jarawa's arrest. Now they're on a tour of world capitals, to drum up support. The third, a gaunt-looking man, was in an ill-fitting jacket without a tie. A white woman was there as well. She was on her feet, talking animatedly and gesticulating, then she abruptly fell silent as I was shown in. A couple of mobile phones lay ostentatiously on the table; beside them was a shiny brochure. I recognized the name on the cover: it was a company Jamie had been looking into in relation to the African arms trade. One of the Renouveau National guys waved his hand and without looking up said, "Later, later. I told you not to disturb us."

The porter showed me into a side room just off the suite. I could still hear the white woman speaking, with occasional interjections from one of the African guys, but it was hard to make out the words. After awhile I gave up trying. Scattered over the floor of the room I was in were piles of new clothes and shopping bags from Knightsbridge boutiques. As I stared at an expensive-looking suit hanging up behind the door, a dream I'd had the night before came back to me. It was about Jarawa. He was at my door in his three-piece suit, pleading with me to pardon him and let him go. I explained that it wasn't me who'd sentenced him but he wouldn't believe me. A horrible sense of guilt had begun to take hold as it dawned on me that perhaps he was right. . . .

A door opened. There was the sound of laughter. The woman was saying, "Well you know, we'll talk about this again," then I could hear the soft ping of the lift doors. I got up and walked through to the main suite. The two guys in suits were in a huddle, talking in low voices. The other man sat apart, staring blankly out the window. There was something about his long face, but what it was didn't click at first, not until we'd finished with the introductions. The man had remained wordless as he shook my hand but his eyes had that same uncomfortable ferocity as his cousin's.

I quickly ran through the campaign presentation. It started

with what Jamie termed "our coup"—the agreement with the other human rights agencies to coordinate efforts under my supervision. I'd already given this same presentation to a group of Labour MPs that morning and a feeling of disengagement invaded me as I mechanically repeated the words. I talked about our media strategy before moving on to lobbying, intelligence, then finally Jarawa's appeal.

I noticed that no one was really paying any attention to me. One guy sat fiddling with his mobile phone and looking at his watch while the other flicked through the brochure the woman had left. Jarawa's cousin still sat apart, not looking at me, not looking at the others, just staring out over a Hyde Park already drenched in summer colors. I stopped speaking for a moment and the two guys in suits glanced up at me almost for the first time. I said I thought the best thing would be to organize a press briefing as soon as possible, for tomorrow afternoon perhaps, with all three of them present. Maybe it would make the greatest impact if Jarawa's cousin spoke.

One of the other guys let out a huge guffaw, "He doesn't speak English! He hardly even speaks French!"

Jarawa's cousin looked briefly to the other two men as they sniggered then turned back to the window. It was obvious that he knew he was being talked about, but his face exuded a prisoner's passivity. There was something of Christian's hangdog look about him too. I remembered the interview with Jarawa I'd read in the library the other day, with that story about the kid with Down's syndrome. It had stuck in the back of my mind for some reason. Did Jarawa's cousin know this story as well? Did he too remember the child? I would have liked to ask him, if there was any way I could.

• • •

That evening the phone rang while I was reading Jessica a bed-
time story. Marianne was in the garden, so I got up to answer it,
with Jessica pulling at my shirt. Before I even picked up the
receiver, though, somehow I knew it was Christian and I had
this visceral desire not to talk to him. I just felt it wouldn't be
good for me.

He sounded pretty desperate, even more so than the other
day when he left that message for me at work. I could hear pub
sounds in the background and his speech was slurred. I can't
understand a word you're saying, I said, just calm down and
speak slowly. I have to see you tonight, he said, there's something
I have to tell you.

"I don't know. It's not really practical right now. Maybe we
can see each other later on in the week."

"Later on in the week? I have to see you tonight. I'm in London. I can come 'round and see you at home. You won't have to
move, I'll come to your house."

"No, where are you? I'll come and meet you."

I didn't want to see Christian, but on the other hand he
couldn't come 'round here. For a start, I'd have to explain to
Marianne about that day—the day I identified Susan Tedeschi's
body I mean. I never told her about it. I never told anybody. I
don't know why.

He gave me the name of a pub in Camden so I said I'd be
there in an hour or so. I hung up and went back to Jessica's
room. She was sort of dozing, lying crosswise on the bed, so I
straightened her out, tucked her in, switched on the lamp on the
chest of drawers and turned out the main light. But she woke up
and called out to me tearfully. I sat down on the bed and put her
on my knee. "What's up," I said, "is it that monster again?"

"It's not a monster. It's a man, I told you before, the man with
the mask. . . . Look what he's done to Teddy!"

She reached down and picked up the teddy bear off the

floor; I had to hold her 'round the waist so she didn't fall off my knee. She was getting all worked up.

"See? See?"

The teddy bear's head is stitched onto its body, and the stitching had come loose and undone in parts. The head crooked to one side in a slightly macabre way. "See? Look what he's trying to do to me too!" She proffered her neck to me. I examined it carefully. "A mark," she said, "a red mark. Can't you see it?"

I couldn't see it. She must have been making it up. I put her back to bed and tucked her in. "If that's all the man with the mask can do then I wouldn't worry too much about him."

I was hungry and I'd thought about taking Christian out to dinner, but as soon as I caught sight of him in the pub I realized there was no chance of that. His face had undergone a remarkable transformation since I'd last seen him. It looked sunken, wrecked, as if it were about to slide off his skull or something. He'd always seemed younger than his age and all of a sudden he looked older, much older. His eyes were drowned and glassy. He'd obviously been drinking for some time and he stared up at me in puzzlement. "You're here!"

I bought a beer and when I got back to the table Christian had pulled himself together a little. He was grinning strangely and putting on a show of small-talk normality. "And how are things going on the Jarawa campaign?"

"It's moving along . . . had a strange meeting today . . . I'm seeing the ambassador tomorrow . . . some military guy. I'm amazed he agreed to meet me . . . Jo's doing well—did you see her on *Newsnight*?"

"No. I don't watch too much TV these days."

"She's doing a fantastic job."

"Great. Fantastic."

I sipped at my beer and gazed around the pub. There wasn't a single woman in it. It was one of those depressing places with dark wood, worn varnish, and greasy green carpets that give off an odor of beer, cigarettes, and urine—exactly the kind of place solitary men go to get drunk.

"You weren't at the funeral."

"No, I wasn't. I'm sorry."

"No need to apologize. I'm no fan of graveyard scenes either." He laughed bleakly and stared at his pint glass. I wondered momentarily if he'd gone mad but didn't say anything. His mind seemed to drift off. "You know when I was young, six or seven years old, we had a little house in the country and it was on the road to a graveyard. . . . I'll never forget the sight of those coffins being hauled along. It was like a scene from the Middle Ages."

"Really?"

"Really."

There was a long pause while I tried to think of something to say, but I couldn't. Christian seemed lost in his memories. "I remember that house in the country. I remember a forest behind it where I once found a hedgehog. I caught it and stuck it in a box. I didn't really know what to do with it though so I just left it there, in the box under my bed—for weeks maybe—until Mum started complaining about the smell. So one evening I opened the lid. Inside was this horrible greenish brown slime. Just the slime and the spines. I can still remember the smell."

A raucous laugh broke out from a table at the other side of the pub and several of the solitary drinkers standing at the bar glanced up from their drinks.

"Listen, Christian. For Christ's sake. You've got to pull yourself together."

Christian stared at me wildly. "Well I can't just pull myself together. I can't just *pull* myself together. Jesus!"

I forced myself to continue. "Look . . . you need help, you

need to open yourself up to help, a doctor, a counsellor, whatever—"

He cut me off. "You don't know the half of it. Not the half of
it." He sat musing and playing with his coaster. "I have no means
of escape. I have to confront myself at every moment. My life is
a mirror I'm not allowed to look away from. If I was an alcoholic
I could drink my way through it. Drink my way to the other
end. I forced myself to drink tonight because I knew I was
meeting you, but normally I can't do it."

I shook my head. "This is getting you absolutely nowhere. I'll
get a cab down to Paddington with you. I'll put you on a train
home."

He didn't seem to hear me though. "The worst is not what
you think. The worst is not even that we loved each other. It was
that Susan . . . Susan and me—"

"Susan was being unfaithful to you."

Christian looked up at me, genuinely surprised. "How did
you know?"

"I didn't know. I guessed. Is that what you got me up here to
tell me?"

"No." We drank in silence for a while, then Christian started
rambling on about his wife. "She met a guy, a younger guy, your
age. It was absurd. I didn't know at first, I didn't have a clue. Anyway Susan got careless, or maybe she wanted me to find out. . . .
I heard her talking on the phone one day when she must have
known I was there. Later I looked through her things and found
a letter, just lying there, not hidden or anything. I couldn't
believe it. So I confronted her with the letter and she admitted
it. I still couldn't believe it. She said she loved me, but that things
had got stale. She needed to get this out of her system and all
that crap. She didn't want to leave me, not at that point anyway.
I should've left her there and then but I didn't. I couldn't. I didn't
have the strength.

"Life went on. The only difference was that I knew everything now. I knew that when she wasn't home with me she was fucking this other guy. In a way it made it much easier for Susan, everything being out in the open like that. She didn't have to hide anything anymore; she didn't have to go through the hassle of secret rendezvous. She could even sleep over at this guy's place now, when before she had to come home every night.

"I should've left her as soon as I found out. If I'd left her then, she'd have come banging at my door. She'd have come back to me eventually and I could have made my choice. She wasn't in love with this other guy. She thought she wanted me but when I didn't dump her, when she saw what I was willing to put up with, she knew I was weak. Then, near the end, I could see I'd lost her. Not because of the other guy, but I'd lost her anyway. She became dismissive of me. She'd grown stronger. I couldn't contemplate her leaving me though. I couldn't contemplate her being alive and not being with me. . . ."

Christian was speaking in a low, robotic voice. I shook my head again. "I don't want to hear any more. I don't want to know these personal things." He stopped, looked quizzically up at me, then continued talking. I interrupted. "I said I didn't want to hear. I don't want to hear it!" I was almost shouting. I was upset, I don't know why. Christian just stared at me in amazement and there was an uneasy minute or two of silence.

Eventually I said, "Look, I'm sorry. I'd like to help out but I honestly can't see what I can do."

"You *do* know what you can do." His stare was unnervingly direct. "You're scared of me. Why are you scared of me?"

"I'm not *scared* of you, for Christ's sake." I looked away in irritation. "I'll get a cab with you to the station."

"There aren't any more trains tonight. They're doing work on the line. The last one went at nine."

"To the coach station then."

Christian put his hand to his chin and kind of slumped in his chair. In the intensity of the encounter I'd forgotten how drunk he actually was. Suddenly, whatever menace he might have posed to me seemed to vanish, to disappear so completely that I wondered just what it was that had upset me in the first place.

Outside, the drizzle had cleared and the wet city glistened in the streetlight. Christian seemed to have developed a stoop since I'd last seen him, or perhaps it was the drink. He kept up a wandering monologue as we walked down Camden High Street. "There'd been a chance maybe . . . we'd shared a bed but I couldn't . . . I hadn't . . ."

I'd changed my mind about the coach station. I remembered a hotel nearby. I'd once spent a night there with a Brazilian woman I'd met in a Soho bar, years ago. In the morning she'd packed her bags and I'd driven her to Heathrow to catch her plane to São Paulo. I could still remember her face and the nakedness of her smile, so different from an Englishwoman's smile.

The reception area was grimly functional and deserted, except for an unshaven Indian-looking guy behind the desk, watching football on a tiny black-and-white television. I got out my wallet but Christian waved his hand. "Don't be absurd." He went through his pockets and fished out a ten-pound note. "What the hell have I done with my Visa?"

"Don't worry about it."

I paid for the room and gave Christian some money for breakfast and to get home with in the morning. Then just as I was about to leave, he seemed to sober up a bit and suddenly came over all apologetic. He said he was really sorry for doing this to me, that he felt humiliated. It's all right, I said, ring me when you've sorted things out a bit.

"Yes, I'll ring you. I need to talk to you. I'll send you a

check." Then, when I'd already left and was on the footpath, he appeared at the hotel window and shouted out again, "I'll ring you! I'll ring you!"

People were spilling out of pubs, talking loudly about where they were going next or how they were getting home. In a way I felt bad about leaving Christian in a hotel, but then on the other hand I was also relieved to be rid of him. I remembered that I hadn't eaten yet and I was still hungry, it was getting on though, and I wondered whether restaurant kitchens would still be open. Then I had another idea. Charlotte lived just around the corner.

I found the art deco block Charlotte's flat is in and pressed her button on the intercom, the door buzzed open before I had time to say who I was. I could see her peering down at me as I climbed the stairs, sizing me up like a club bouncer. "What the hell are *you* doing here?" She'd messily pulled a jumper over her underwear and a television blared in the background.

Charlotte let me in then disappeared into the bedroom. I poured some wine and helped myself to the cold pasta salad on the dinner table. As I ate, my mind drifted back to the meeting I'd had with the people from Renouveau National. I remembered one of the men smiling at me and saying, "Well you know, politics in our country is a dangerous business." I'd replied, "But what's at issue is not the death of one man . . . not one man, do you see?" It was only now that I realized I'd unconsciously used Christian's words, from the day his wife had died.

Charlotte was talking to someone on the phone in the bedroom but I could only catch snippets of what she was saying: ". . . no, really, I'm tired tonight . . . I wouldn't be any fun . . . yeah I'll see you tomorrow night . . . you too." She threw open the bedroom door. She'd put on some makeup and a pretty pink shirt with a flower pattern. "It's good to see you and everything but don't ever just turn up here again unannounced. Okay?"

We had some wine and a late supper and chatted idly. After awhile we started kissing across the table, then we lay down on the sofa and continued talking, laughing, kissing, joking around. At the same time I was kind of playing with the buttons of her shirt, undoing them slowly, waiting for the conversation to dissolve.

We'd been talking about our jobs and at one point Charlotte said, "What's your real ambition in life? What's the one thing you want to do before you die?"

"I'm aiming for immortality."

"No seriously, what's your ambition? What do you want to do with your life?"

I stopped messing about for a moment and sat up. "I don't know . . . an international posting . . . the UN, maybe Paris, maybe UNESCO . . . I want to move on, move up, pretty soon."

"So does everyone. What I mean is, isn't there something that engrosses you, something you must achieve?"

"I don't have that kind of ambition." I thought again. "There are things . . . there's the campaign I told you about—"

"You mean the guy they're going to execute?"

"Yeah."

"So it's your job after all. That's your real interest, your job."

"No. I couldn't give a damn about my job."

We were silent for a moment. Somehow the atmosphere had changed.

Eventually I said, "I had this strange encounter just now," and then I found myself telling Charlotte about meeting up with Christian.

When I finished, Charlotte lit a cigarette and said, "Let me get this straight. A friend rings you up. He wants to talk to you about his wife's death, presumably he wants a bit of emotional support. So you end up dumping him in a hotel 'round the corner?"

"He's not a friend. He's just a colleague."

"So what? He's a human being, isn't he?"

"I didn't want the sordid details. I didn't want to know about his wife screwing some other guy."

"Why not? Too close to home?"

I didn't say anything for a while. Charlotte stared at me defiantly.

I said, "Why are you seeing me? What's in it for you?"

"Why am I fucking you, you mean?"

"Yes."

"Does it matter? I like the way you look. I like your face. I like your body."

"That's all there is to it? I'm some kind of sex object?"

"Why not?"

She looked at me with amusement as she did up the buttons I'd undone on her shirt. I got up off the couch.

"I've got to go. Thanks for dinner. Shall I give you a call sometime during the week?"

"Why not?"

I kissed her on the forehead and she said, "Give my regards to Marianne." I could hear her switching the TV back on as I walked down the stairs to the main entrance.

I got a cab home. It was Monday night and apart from a few other cabs there was hardly any traffic on the streets. London looked shabby and beautiful in its enormous emptiness, like a vast illuminated scrubland. I thought about Charlotte then I thought about Christian and his dead hedgehog. A childhood memory returned to me of a summer in the country. My cousin Peter had constructed a crossbow and we'd gone to the nearby woods and killed a rabbit—I can still recall its jerky, struggling death. I hadn't thought about my childhood for a long time. I had the sensation it was something that had in fact happened to someone else and not to me at all.

The bedroom door was shut but the light was still on. I didn't go in immediately though. Instead I went to the little room we use as an office, on the other side of the house. We've got a filing cabinet in there, for documents to do with the house, tax returns, birth certificates, that kind of stuff. There are also files full of Marianne's personal stuff, although I'd never looked at them before. That's what I wanted to look at now. Seeing Christian had given me stupid ideas.

Everything was arranged tidily, a file for old letters, a file for exhibition programmes, a file for this, a file for that. There were essays she'd written as a student in that typically rounded French handwriting. There were notebooks too, clearly labeled 1998, 1999, 2000, etc. They looked like diaries. I'd never known she'd kept a diary, never seen one about the house. I flicked through the one for last year. Some of the entries were in French, some in English, some a mix of the two. I read a few at random. Mostly they were about her work: "Big canvas. Thought I might move on to love but no it seems I'm stuck with this fear." There were notes about Jessica's development: "Her linguistic skills different in French and English. English vocabulary wider but grasp of grammatical structure not as good as in French." I skimmed through to find any mention of me, but in vain. I noticed that she'd marked every third or fourth entry with an asterisk. I wondered what that meant.

When I went into the bedroom Marianne was lying on her stomach on the bed, barefoot but fully dressed, reading. We had a shower together then Marianne said let's smoke—she'd got some stuff from Jake and Natalie. As I rolled I said, are you sure you should be smoking when you're pregnant? She looked up at me in surprise. I want to be out of it, she said, then I want to make love. We smoked the joint. We started talking: Marianne said, "There's something I've been thinking about over the last few days, it's somehow to do with being pregnant again—this summer I really want us to get married."

I began to feel warm and relaxed. I said, "I want to get married too."

Marianne started to get all excited about the idea, "We could go down to my father's place. We could get married at that little church in Montargues, I'd like that."

I remembered last summer at Montargues, watching Marianne and Jessica swimming in the river. I remembered being in bed with Marianne that night, the fresh smell of river mud still on our bodies.

"I'd like that too."

By the time we'd smoked the second joint it seemed like we were too stoned to make love. We lay on the bed on our sides, just looking at each other and not touching. Marianne was past the talkative stage and now looked pretty gone. Contradictory feelings of passion and detachment washed through me. The butterfly palpitations of an artery on her wrist fascinated me. After an age of silence and gazing at each other I finally said I thought I was too stoned to get an erection. Marianne said, "You've got one already."

We made love for a long time. I'd woken up that morning with a powerful desire for her, I now remembered. It had remained with me throughout the day, had simmered on through the meeting with Christian, had fed my annoyance with him, my intolerance of him. Afterward I got up and opened the window and then lay back down on the bed again. There was a cool night breeze and I could feel it caressing my body—it almost felt like we were still making love, although Marianne was by now asleep beside me.

She was on her back now and I tried to make out the curve of our second child in her belly, but I couldn't. I thought about getting married, I realized that I actually wanted to, for the first time in my life. Things had changed. I wouldn't see Charlotte again. I wouldn't do anything to harm my relationship with Marianne. I would do everything to nurture it.

V

THAT DOPE WAS STRONG. I GOT UP LATER THAN USUAL AND WAS STILL at the breakfast table when Marianne got back from dropping Jessica off at the day care center. "I'm going to work at home for a few hours," I said—I had that meeting with the ambassador in Kensington at one so there was no point in going all the way into the office first. Marianne seemed sort of disconcerted but I didn't think anything of it. She wandered about the kitchen restlessly, vaguely tidying up, putting things away more or less at random. "You're not working in the studio this morning?" I asked. We bought this house partly on account of the big shed in the back garden, which Marianne's converting into a studio. "Yes . . . no . . . I don't know," Marianne replied.

I scanned the copy of the *Guardian* Marianne had brought back. Somewhere on page four or five were a couple of para-

graphs about Jarawa's wife. She's English and she'd arrived in the
U.K. unexpectedly the night before. She made no comment on
arrival at Heathrow, where she was picked up by a member of
the family. It was a brief article and I recognized Jo's writing
style—it's not so rare that a journalist simply copies a press
release, word for word. There was a small photo, not recent, of a
stylish-looking white woman with wavy blond hair.

I started going through work stuff at the breakfast table and
after about half an hour Marianne came back in to tell me she
had to go up to Primrose Hill, a Belgian dealer had made an
appointment. She seemed nervous. I heard the front door slam-
ming and I glanced out of the kitchen window, which looks out
into the street. Marianne had her head down and was walking
with brisk, tiny steps. I got up, opened the front door and looked
down the street. She was standing on the corner. A cab went by.
Marianne hailed it and it stopped. It was unlike her to take cabs
in the middle of the day.

I went back inside, put the kettle on, sat down at the table,
glanced at the page in front of me, then got up again. A sun ray,
reflected off our new cooker, caught me in the eye and I had to
look away. I went into the bedroom and stood for a moment in
the middle of the room. Marianne's handbag sat on her dressing
table: she'd taken her purse with her but had left her handbag. I
picked it up, opened it, and in one violent action emptied the
contents onto the bed. A pile of odds and ends lay scattered over
the duvet—lipstick, makeup, Tampax, a book of stamps, coins, a
shopping list, a passport-sized photo of Jessica, an old plane ticket
to Montpellier. I glanced at it all then put everything back. I let
out my breath: I'd been unaware I'd been holding it in. She'd
know I'd gone through her handbag of course—things would be
in the wrong place. I wondered if she'd mention it to me or not.

The phone was on the floor instead of where it normally is,
which is on the bedside table. I picked up the receiver and hit the

redial button. There was a recorded message from customer inquiries, Paddington station, "Your call has been placed in a queue." I put down the receiver and sat down on the floor beside the phone, thinking, listening to the whistle of the kettle, as insistent as a baby's cry. Even as I put my shoes on and found my keys I was telling myself how stupid I was. I was telling myself I didn't know what I was going to do but I seemed to be doing it anyway.

For a while I wandered aimlessly about the concourse. Even well past peak hour the station was teeming with people and I knew there wasn't much chance of finding Marianne, even if she was there. Eventually it struck me that the one thing I didn't want was for Marianne to see me before I saw her, so I went and stood behind a magazine stand in W.H. Smith. I'd picked up some magazine and was flicking through it when this bulky-looking guy approached me. "Excuse me—I don't know if you remember me . . . we talked at the AMSA seminar a couple of weeks ago."

I remembered him. He was one of those desperadoes who hang around NGO conferences hustling for money—he'd harangued me for half an hour about some documentary he was trying to get funding for. It was about executions that had gone wrong. People who'd survived being hanged, electrocutions that sent flames shooting through people's heads, that kind of thing. Now here he was again, pitching the same idea as I scanned the station over his shoulder, my eyes swiveling around the concourse for a glimpse of Marianne. But at the same time I was thinking about Jessica for some reason. I was thinking about her teddy bear whose head was coming loose. It was bugging me— it'd been on my mind when I'd woken up that morning.

Then suddenly I thought I saw Marianne. It wasn't so much the back of her head that I recognized, more the way she moved, those tiny steps. The guy was in my line of vision and I had to move over to one side to see better. The woman I thought was Marianne briefly inclined her head in my direction and for a second or two I got a clear view of her silhouetted face and bridgeless nose. I began to feel funny and light-headed, the way I feel sometimes just before I have to make a speech in public. I hadn't really expected to see her here after all, I realized.

The man had shoved a card into my hands. It was the kind you get printed up in machines in train stations. He was saying, "I could come and see you next week. I can bring you the written proposal and we can discuss this."

"I don't know . . . maybe."

"I've seen your name in the paper . . . that diplomat who's been sentenced to death, right?"

"Yeah."

"It's just that I happen to know something about him. Might interest you. Maybe we can talk about it."

"Yeah. I'm sorry. Got to go, I've got a train."

"Shall I call you?"

"Sure, call me."

I'd lost Marianne and began struggling through the crowd in the direction I'd seen her walking. Then I caught sight of her again, much closer than I'd expected: if she'd turned 'round at that exact moment she definitely would have seen me. That panicked me a little and I dropped back. In any case I could clearly see where she was headed now. I glanced up at the indicator board. The 11:38 from Oxford was arriving on platform twelve. It was gliding into the station as Marianne made her way to meet it. That was why she'd been in such a hurry, of course. She'd almost got there too late.

I hid by the Tie Rack shop and could see her only from the back. She was wearing jeans and the cashmere sweater I gave her last Christmas. Even in jeans she managed to look groomed and well dressed. She looked good and I felt stupidly proud of her. I could tell she was nervous by the way she was pacing on the spot, scanning the crowd of alighting passengers. She was afraid of missing whoever it was she was waiting for, and that meant the person didn't know she was there.

Then suddenly she started gesticulating. A man came into view. He was tall, middle-aged, slightly overweight and his hair was thinning. I couldn't see Marianne's face but the man's was beaming. He hugged her and I could see them talking animatedly. Perhaps she was explaining why she'd come to the station. Perhaps the original plan had been for him to pick her up at the house. The man's hand was against Marianne's lower back and then at one moment it seemed to brush down by her buttocks. The memory of the last time I'd seen him seemed to explode onto my consciousness with a bizarre force, as if it had been impatiently waiting all this time to explain my idiocy to me.

I followed them through a labyrinth of scaffolding and hanging green canvas and cordons. The man was quite a bit taller than Marianne and had his arm protectively 'round her shoulder as they continued to talk. It was the first time I'd ever tried to tail someone and it took me a little while to get the hang of it. If I dropped too far back I was afraid I'd lose them, but when I got close there was the chance that Marianne would turn 'round—I concentrated on getting the tactical trade-off right.

Then, just as we reached the tube entrance, I got a shock. Climbing up the stairs into the main station was Christian. I'd forgotten about him. I'd forgotten that he'd probably end up at Paddington this morning to catch his train back home. We'd talked only the night before, but an era had passed since then. In the two or three minutes since I'd seen Marianne embrace the man on the platform I'd already become a different person—I could feel the change moving through my body like a drug. It was disconcerting but fascinating and I wondered where exactly it would take me.

Christian seemed changed as well. Last night he'd been drunk, shuffling and incoherent. Now there was a vague determination to his movements. His shirt, which had been badly crumpled, was freshly ironed and his long, lank hair was neatly combed and tied back. His face still looked kind of wrecked, but somehow less catastrophically so than the night before. He looked up as he got to the top of the stairs and we stared at each other—I could sense a disturbing intimacy in his gaze. It was hard to read this expression of his that seemed somehow quizzical, as though I had something to answer for. He stopped for no more than a second or two and so did I. Then we walked past each other wordlessly.

A tube pulled in to the Circle line platform. The doors snapped open and the two of them moved toward the carriage. I scuttled out of my hiding place behind the vending machine and into the next carriage—I'd been dreading this moment when I would be at my most vulnerable. The thing is, I couldn't imagine what kind of confrontation Marianne and I could possibly have right now, what we could possibly say to each other. I kept an eye on them through the windows that separated the two carriages. They were sitting opposite each other, saying nothing now, maybe smiling at each other; it was hard to see. My heart was jolting strangely inside me and I took deep breaths to calm myself. I was sweating intensely. The image of Christian's quizzical face came back to me. I could feel an anger surge up in me, and yet it wasn't particularly directed at Marianne or her lover. For some reason it was Christian who was the object of this peculiar fury.

They got out at High Street Kensington and I waited until the last moment to jump onto the platform. A group of Japanese tourists blocked the entrance and in the confusion I lost sight of Marianne and the man. I really thought I'd missed them altogether and felt an odd relief that I didn't have to follow them anymore. Then over the sea of camcorders and baseball caps I suddenly caught a glimpse of the man's head—he's tall, taller than me. A tour guide herded the Japanese tourists into a tube that had pulled in on the other side of the platform. Marianne and the man were on the stairs now and I could see them quite clearly.

I followed them to a square somewhere north of the High Street. There was a preppy pub on the corner, someone had taken me there once years ago. It was the kind of place public-school boys and girls with year-round tans went to get drunk in. It was the kind of place I'd never have taken Marianne to. There was a garden out front and Marianne sat down at a table there while the guy went in to order drinks and food. She was on her own again. She started stroking her hair, patting it into place. I knew exactly what was going through her mind; I knew her so well. She was thinking: I want to check my makeup and hair but I don't have my compact with me, and I can't get up and go to the toilet until he comes back, otherwise we might lose the table.

I went into the little park on the square. Two dogs were copulating in a sandpit in the children's play area while a few kids looked on. I sat down over the other side of the park, on a bench partially hidden by a ragged bush. I could peer through it with the near certainty that Marianne wouldn't be able to see me. There was little danger of her looking my way in any case; the two of them barely took their eyes off each other. I was safe in that regard and that meant that I could relax for the first time since I'd spotted her on the concourse. My thoughts spurted ahead of me incoherently. I wondered where they slept together, whether the man was married, whether he'd ever been to our home. I was afraid of what would happen after their lunch at the pub. No doubt I'd follow them to some block of flats 'round the corner and then I'd find myself alone again, abandoned to my imagination.

Marianne and the man had been served lunch but they continued talking between mouthfuls as though it was not in their power to stop the tide of conversation, even to eat. It was strange to see Marianne garrulous like that when normally she's quite sparing with her words. I remembered how different Charlotte had seemed on an intimate level compared with Marianne, that first time we'd slept together, and it struck me with even greater force how unfamiliar Marianne was to me now. It was as if there were a stranger inhabiting her that she'd never normally let me see.

An electronic blare seemed to burst up from beneath me, jerking my concentration away from Marianne. It took me a few startled moments to realize that it was my mobile phone. I fumbled clumsily with it in my state of heightened tension.

"Jamie here. Listen, where the fuck are you? I've got the ambassador's secretary on hold. He's wondering when the hell you're going to show up."

I glanced at my watch. I'd forgotten about my appointment with the ambassador. I was already half an hour late. I'd have canceled any other appointment, but it had been such extraordinary luck to get the ambassador to see me in the first place that I couldn't back out of it now.

"Sorry. I'm stuck in a traffic jam. Tell him I'll be there in fifteen minutes."

I switched the mobile off and shoved it back in my pocket. Marianne and the man were finishing up, in any case. What was it that they were talking about with such passion? It was like watching a TV program in a foreign language where you can sense the emotions but not understand the plot. This feeling of being a voyeur was entirely new to me. I'd always been one of those people who regard themselves as inside life, never on the outside.

The sun was streaming through the bushes and the day was warming up. I watched as Marianne suddenly pulled her cashmere sweater over her head in a single liquid movement. Underneath she was wearing a halter top I didn't recognize. It looked good on her—revealing clothes like that suit her Mediterranean skin. She looked sexy in fact, and a curious aching feeling I'd never experienced before crawled through me.

VI

AROUND A DOZEN POLICEMEN WERE STANDING 'ROUND OUTSIDE the embassy, their walkie-talkies exploding into a crackle of voices every few seconds. What's happening, I asked one of them. There's going to be a protest here this afternoon, he said, I'm afraid that's all I know, sir. I went up to the main entrance and was searched by a security guard. I was wondering who'd organized the protest, it took my mind off things. I wondered why I hadn't heard about it and that irritated me. I was supposed to be co-ordinating the Jarawa campaign. Anyone organizing a protest should have got in touch with me.

The guard showed me into a small, stuffy reception room at the back of the building. It had been done out like the study of a Victorian anthropologist. African masks hung down from the picture railings and two small wooden statues of squat men with huge penises and screaming mouths stared at a hagiographic portrait of the president, opposite. I barely had time to take all this in before a burly guy in his mid-forties, an embassy official of some sort, came in with a pile of documents. He was dressed in a pale gray suit and dark red tie. I also noticed a handkerchief peeking out of his breast pocket. It seemed somehow out of place, at odds with the man's beefy build and shaved head. It reminded me of that photo of Jarawa and his fob watch.

"Do you speak French?"

"I can read it."

"Good. The ambassador has already gone to his lunch appointment but his secretary left these documents for you to look over. You can make notes if you wish. I'll leave you the documents for thirty minutes then I'll be back to answer any questions you may have."

The guy left. I glanced through the papers. They were faxed copies of court digests, police reports, all kinds of stuff. They seemed to be mainly about a triple murder Jarawa was supposed to have ordered last year on the twenty-first of December. The trouble was that I couldn't concentrate on the documents at all. Once I was by myself again a wave of confused thought seemed to swamp my mind. Flashes from this morning came back to me. I remembered Marianne in the kitchen, looking anxious, saying she had to go and meet a Belgian dealer at Joseph Kimberly. I'd never caught her lying to me before and I'd naïvely imagined that she never had. What struck me here was the detail of the fictional dealer's nationality. Why Belgian and not American or Japanese, or even French or German? Or would those have been too likely and thus less believable? In any case it seemed a strange choice, the baroque touch of someone who was getting a kick out of the situation.

The guy came back in. Thirty minutes had apparently passed, although it felt like five. The room was uncomfortably warm and I could feel sweat beading on my forehead. I hadn't really digested any of the information in the documents.

Did I have any questions, he asked. Yes, I replied and I tried hard to think of something to say. All that came to me was that I was hungry, that it was past lunchtime and I hadn't had anything to eat since the piece of toast that morning. Finally I asked why I was being shown these documents now and why they hadn't been released earlier. The man said there'd been a lot of confusion arising from the fact that the trial had been held in camera, but what Monsieur Jarawa had actually been sentenced for was complicity in the murder of three businessmen. He'd been defended by a French lawyer and convicted by a jury and a French-trained judge. The man said he wanted to stress this point, since there'd been so much speculation over the supposed political motivation of the sentence.

I said, so in other words what you're saying is that he's just a common criminal; he's being put to death on account of an ordinary crime. The man smiled at me. He's been convicted of murder and has been sentenced accordingly, he replied. If it's the death penalty that particularly upsets you then why single us out? Why demand sanctions against us and not the United States?

Our contention is that he's a political prisoner, I replied, trying to sound as indignant as possible. Even when I was unprepared, as I often was, I was used to holding my own in this kind of confrontation. But I could feel the words slipping away from me, slipping toward this clever bureaucrat with his French-inflected Oxbridge accent and his slick rhetoric. He continued to talk, but because it had become so stiflingly hot in the little room I was finding it difficult to concentrate on his words. He leaned forward conspiratorially: In fact there are a lot of influential people working behind the scenes to get Monsieur Jarawa's sentence commuted, he was saying, but this work could easily be compromised by pressure from Western governments and organizations.

The government could well react adversely to interference from the West.

The official walked me back through the embassy to the front entrance. He put his hand on my shoulder and I could feel the dampness of my shirt. Of course I know Monsieur Jarawa quite well, he continued, as many of us in the diplomatic service do. He has a great sense of humor and his wife is a very beautiful woman. He and the ambassador are very friendly too. I can assure you that I'm personally doing all I can for Monsieur Jarawa. We used to go to galleries together, you know, when he was in London. He loves contemporary art!

We'd reached the entrance. The protest outside the embassy had already got under way—thirty or forty people were holding up placards and chanting. The embassy official made a great show of shaking my hand warmly in full view of the protesters and I walked down the stairs and out the gate. I tried to make my way through the crowd of people, but it was difficult. They were encircling me then began chanting even more insistently. One guy in particular who looked nineteen or twenty stood right next to me and started shouting about murderers. He was accusing me of being complicit in a murder or being a murderer, I don't know which. He was shouting in my ear so that I couldn't hear anything else and piercing me with his accusing stare. What with the stuffiness of the room I'd been in and now the shouting I was beginning to feel dizzy. He was standing in my way and I felt hot and closed in and I sort of pushed at him and he pushed me back onto the gates, quite hard. I thought he might hit me. Then I heard a policeman say, "Okay, Okay, let the gentleman pass." The young guy kept shouting and staring at me but he didn't push me again and the policeman cleared the way so that I could get back from the embassy gates.

I thanked the policeman and walked quickly away, in no particular direction. At one point I got out my mobile to make sure it was switched off—I didn't want any calls. I should have gone straight to the office of course and worked out a press release with Jo and written up a report, but I didn't feel like it. For one thing I'd fucked up the whole encounter. I hadn't seen the ambassador. Then there was the letter signed by all the academics that I was supposed to have delivered. And I'd also been meaning to raise the matter of the visa applications I'd made for Jo and a volunteer, which had been rejected for no apparent reason. But I'd been comprehensively outmaneuvered and hadn't even found out who it was I'd spoken to. Worst of all, I'd messed up the documents business. I hadn't taken any notes; I couldn't remember a damn thing that was in them. The stupid thing was I could have easily stolen the more important ones. I could have slipped them into my wallet; they were only faxes printed on thermal paper.

Later I found myself back at the pub, the one where Marianne and the man had had lunch. I remembered the smile I'd seen her give him there, a smile that so patently hid nothing that it made me feel sick. They were long gone of course. I was hungry so I ordered a beer and a sandwich, but the barmaid told me the food was finished so I had a couple of packets of crisps instead. I drank a beer then had another one. A flat, nightmarish air of mid-afternoon seediness hung about the pub. Beside me at the bar, two young male doctors were getting drunk after a shift, exchanging medical horror stories: "They'd brought in this guy who'd had a hang-gliding accident. His testicles had been badly crushed and Steve had to, well, surgically castrate him to stop the hemorrhaging. . . ."

I ended up getting a bus to Paddington, where I'd left the car. It was ages since I'd last caught a bus. I climbed upstairs and sat right at the front, like I used to do when I was a child, and waited for the conductor to come up, but they didn't seem to have conductors on this route anymore. I rubbed the grime from the window and looked out over the streets of West London. It occurred to me that Jarawa probably knew these streets too, and that although I'd never been to his city he'd certainly been to mine. So in some sense we shared a topography. I recalled what the embassy official had said about Jarawa, the personal details I mean—his sense of humor, how they'd gone to art galleries together. All this struck me as odd and at first I couldn't see why. Then after a while I began to understand. On one level I was organizing a campaign to get Jarawa's death sentence commuted. But on another level I'd already kind of written him off as dead, or perhaps as someone who'd never been alive. It was as if he were simply an idea. It had been weird to hear the embassy guy talk about him in the present tense. It had been weird to hear about Jarawa as someone with a sense of humor who liked going to art galleries. And it was weird too to think that he had a wife, who was now in the U.K., probably somewhere in London in fact, not half an hour from where I was.

A middle-aged woman with gray-white roots got on at Knightsbridge and sat down next to me, although there were plenty of other empty seats. She took out a large photo album from her imitation leather bag, extracted a pencil from her coat pocket, and started to write in the album. It couldn't have been easy, because the bus kept shuddering and stopping and then starting again suddenly. She seemed to be writing captions under the photos stuck in the album. They weren't recent photos: judging from the garish colors and white frames they dated from the sixties or early seventies. Most of them were of the same man, in his thirties. He had thick eyebrows and a lick of dark hair over his eyes. The woman was frowning, concentrating on her curious task. What was she writing? Whatever it was, it seemed clear to me that it was something sad, oppressively sad, and I looked away.

• • •

I went home, eventually. Marianne was listening to the radio and shelling peas in the kitchen—it's one of the few things she likes about English produce. She said, "I thought you were going to pick up Jessica. When I got home there was a message from the day care center on the answering machine saying no one had picked her up and I had to go along. I had to get a cab."

It was true I'd said I'd pick her up. It was a bad thing to forget: one of the day care center supervisors would have had to stay behind with Jessica until Marianne had shown up. It put me on the wrong foot and I started apologizing, but Marianne said, "It's okay, I understand, don't worry about it." I noticed that she'd changed her clothes: she wasn't wearing the cashmere sweater and jeans anymore. It was the kind of thing I wouldn't have particularly noticed before, but it set me thinking now. Of course, she'd have had a shower and changed when she got home, I thought. After all, I showered and changed after seeing Charlotte.

We had dinner then I went into the lounge and put the television on. I was tired, incredibly tired. Jessica came into the lounge and clambered up onto my knees, but I was too tired to entertain her. I looked into her face and tried to see myself in it. People have often commented on how much she looks like me but it's the kind of thing people would say anyway. Now, in spite of my tiredness, I wanted to be able to look at her and see my genes at work. Instead, all I could make out was Marianne's nose and skin color. Jessica was playing a new game she'd invented only a few days before, feeling my pockets and trying to guess what I had in them, then reaching in and pulling everything out.

I said, "Where's Teddy? Why don't you get Teddy?"

"No."

"Why not?"

"Teddy's ill."

"Well why don't you go and get Teddy and I'll see if I can make him better."

"No!"

"Go on, Jessica. Go and fetch Teddy."

"No!"

She screamed it out, then scrambled off my knees. We haven't been getting on so well lately, for some reason. She's got this new trick now, where she speaks to me in French and refuses to speak in English. She's quite aware my French isn't up to it—in fact, she deliberately speaks more quickly to make sure I won't understand. It really pisses me off. Marianne says don't show you're pissed off by it, because that'll just encourage her. What annoys me is that it's Marianne who actively encourages her. They speak almost exclusively in French together now. I had it out with Marianne the other day. She got quite angry about it. She'd said: I want Jessica to be completely bilingual and if I don't speak to her in French she'll lose it. I'd shouted: You want her to *be* French, don't you, you can't stand the idea of Jessica being English! I'd stormed out of the house to cool off in the pub. When I'd got back from the pub Marianne had been in an icy mood. She'd said: If you've got anything to say to me you say it calmly, or you say it when Jessica's not around. I don't want Jessica to hear us arguing. I don't want Jessica to hear you raise your voice with me.

Anyway Marianne came into the lounge now and carted Jessica off to bed, while I stared at the television without watching it. I could feel my mind grinding through the events of the day, chaotically analyzing, spewing forth senseless questions, spurious connections. Then eventually Marianne came back with a bottle of wine and a couple of glasses. It's a ritual. After we've got Jessica off to bed we knock off a bottle of wine together. Being pregnant doesn't seem to have stopped Marianne drinking, although sometimes I try to persuade her not to. That night I couldn't be bothered. I didn't even know anymore if the child she was carrying was mine.

Marianne started talking about getting married, was I really serious about it? I said I was. In a bizarre way I meant it too. I was so tired, I was almost under the spell of the ordinariness of everything—it was as if today's events were quite a separate affair that had no relevance to my domestic existence. It was the way I sometimes felt about people being killed in Africa. Marianne was saying she thought late July or early August would be the perfect time, that we could ask just a few friends down to Montargues for the wedding—Jake and Natalie, Claudine, Johnny—then have a big party when we got back. What did I think? I nodded. I may go down to Montargues the weekend after next then, she continued, there'll be a lot to organize. The priest will be a pain, he's not going to like it that we've already got Jessica. She went on in this vein for a while. At some point she repeated: Well what do you think? About what, I asked. Marianne seemed vaguely annoyed: If we're going to get married I want you to be involved too, she said. I want it to be us together organizing everything, not just me. Yeah I know, I replied, it's just that I'm a bit knackered tonight. . . . Anyway how did it go with the Belgian dealer? I'm not sure, Marianne answered, it was some guy from Antwerp. . . . Sally Jacobs had told him to come and see my stuff. . . . He seemed taken with the circle series, you know the one I mean? Yeah, I know the one you mean, I replied.

I'd watched her carefully as she spoke. It interested me how she'd been able to weave a whole narrative in just a few casual words; it was quite an artistic achievement. I wondered whether she'd worked out what she was going to say in advance or whether it had just come out like that, spontaneously, as it were. I could hear Jessica crying. You go, I said, I'm just not getting on with her at the moment.

VII

LATELY I'VE BEEN SPENDING A FAIR AMOUNT OF TIME OUTSIDE A block of flats in Holland Road in West Kensington, where Marianne and her lover rent a bedsit. I follow Marianne there maybe two or three mornings a week. I can sense at the breakfast table whether she's going to meet the guy that day or not. Sometimes I can even sense it the night before. What amazes me is how before I'd failed so comprehensively to pick up on all the little signals that seem so blindingly clear to me now.

I've discovered the man's name, but I don't seem to be interested in finding out much more about him. I suppose I know everything I need to know. I probably knew everything the moment I first saw him. It's his middle-aged ordinariness that troubles me most. If he'd been some handsome young guy perhaps I could have forgiven Marianne. No, that's not quite right.

There aren't any circumstances in which I can imagine forgiving her, but at least I could have understood her better. I've thought about this a great deal. The problem for me is that the man is just so unlike myself. I'm young and physically in good shape, but in the end that works against me. They're the visible advantages that are so easy to dismiss, precisely because of their visibility. What Marianne's lover has is hidden, enigmatic, in the end far more potent. I watch his face as he talks to Marianne and it's quite clear that this is a man you could trust—that even I could trust.

I know which window is theirs; I can see it from the pavement. Sometimes I catch glimpses of them moving around. Once I saw Marianne semi-naked and I was overwhelmed again by the peculiar aching feeling I'd experienced watching them have lunch in the pub. More often than not though they draw the curtains—Charlotte used to draw the curtains too before we went to bed those afternoons. I tend to take this as my cue to leave. Mostly I go straight to work, but sometimes I go for a swim first. I'm not sure why. Perhaps I feel as if I can get rid of something in the pool. But that doesn't seem to work anymore, not in this case anyway. The swimming tires me out though and helps me get through the day. I suppose that's good.

Things have changed at work as well. I've let Jo take over a lot of the things I used to do. I don't work the phones anymore for example, or at least not the way I used to. I haven't been canvassing Labour MPs; I haven't been going to the meetings; I haven't been playing squash with Jamie. The Jarawa case still preoccupies me, but in a different kind of way. There are things that mystify me. When I was first put in charge of the campaign I'd had this idea that I could save a man's life; now I feel more helpless.

I think about him often—when I'm not thinking about Marianne, that is. Before, I might have been interested in the politics of it all, but now that seems tangential. If you're going to be put to death what does it matter why? Surely your mind would be focused on that point in the near future when you will be no more. You'd be looking forward in a way, and not back to how you got where you were. That's how I see it anyway. I sit at my desk and wonder what it must be like for him, in a prison cell and preparing to die. Would there be a constant tension and anxiety or would that dissipate after a while? Would it come and go? Would there be hope? Would you end up getting used to the situation, in the way that ordinary people can seemingly get used to anything?

I've got used to things that would have been completely unimaginable not so long ago. After the initial shock of finding out about Marianne I'd been fairly clear as to what I would do. I would leave her of course, but on my own terms, in my own way, engineered so that I would get the maximum benefit out of the separation. Jessica was certainly a problem and there was the house as well. Everything was very complicated. But I had the upper hand since I knew about her lover and she didn't yet know I knew. However things haven't panned out as they might have, or at least not yet in any case. I started following Marianne and now it's difficult to see the way forward. I think about Christian sometimes and his faithless wife and how he lost her. I wonder why he hasn't called me and what exactly it was he'd wanted to say to me. I realize that my immediate response, to leave Marianne, was a vestige of my old self, the one I sloughed off at Paddington station. What Marianne's infidelity has brought me is a sense of the complexity of things. It occurs to me that in some strange way separation might merely be another way of being together.

Yesterday the routine was a little different. Marianne caught the tube to High Street Ken as usual, but then instead of walking down to Holland Road she turned right and went up to Kensington Park. It wasn't so easy to follow her in the park—I was too exposed—and I contemplated abandoning the chase. And yet I was intrigued; I couldn't leave it alone. I let her walk a long way ahead until I could only just make her out and then I set out after her. That way I could be sure she wouldn't spot me and if I lost her, then too bad. She continued walking way to the east. Then finally I saw where she was headed. She was going to the Serpentine Gallery. I wondered why she'd got the tube to High Street and not to somewhere closer. I spend a lot of time wondering about these matters, the logistics of Marianne's affair.

Anyway, she went into the gallery. I waited behind a tree by the road nearby that cuts through the park. She was in the gallery a good while and eventually came out again with her lover—he must have already been inside before she'd arrived. He had a wicker basket with him: they were going to have a picnic in the park. It was warm and sunny, the guy's jacket was flapping gently in the breeze. He put the basket down, got out a blanket, spread it on the ground and Marianne lay down on the grass. Normally I would have left at this point—it seems that I have to know whether she's with the man or not, but generally my curiosity stops there. However this time I couldn't move: the tree I was hiding behind was too close and Marianne almost certainly would have seen me.

As I watched them I remembered the last time I'd come to this park, not so far from this spot, that day Christian's wife was killed. I remembered the extraordinary feeling of well-being that had surprised me, had washed over me, and just the memory of it brought a little of it back, but not much of it, and not for long, just the time to realize how far I'd traveled since then. They'd finished eating and Marianne was lying down with her head in the man's lap. She was wearing a white T-shirt and the man had pulled it up a little to expose her belly—her slightly swollen belly. He put his hand on it then she put her hand on top of his. The meaning was clear enough.

I hadn't really seen them together, not since that first day when I'd followed them to the pub in Kensington. Normally I would just watch them embrace then disappear into the bedsit on Holland Road. Or sometimes she would go into the building by herself—either he'd already be there or he'd arrive shortly afterward. I'd looked through Marianne's handbag one night for the keys she used to get into the Holland Road building, but I hadn't found them. She keeps them apart from her house and car keys. She must hide them somewhere. That fact made me feel good for some reason. It made me feel she was doing something because of me, that it required some effort to hide her liaison from me and that she felt it was worth the effort.

Anyway, I watched them now, her head in his lap. What struck me was how at ease they seemed to be with each other, how unlike a clandestine relationship it was. Perhaps it was the sexual urgency that was missing. When Charlotte and I met up, for example, it was never more than a few minutes before we had to touch each other, start to undress each other. Marianne and her lover, on the other hand, looked like a happily married couple expecting their second child. How long had they been together? Years, perhaps? I wondered when and how they'd met. Then I remembered how Marianne and I had first met, on a beach in Portugal. These things have no deeper sense, I said to myself. Again, the thought passed through my mind that perhaps I could have forgiven Marianne a quick fling, but not this. Again I corrected myself. Of course, there could be no grounds for forgiveness.

Eventually they got up and wandered off in an easterly direction, which meant they weren't going to the bedsit in Holland Road after all. They walked right by the tree where I was hiding, and I had to slowly curl 'round it so Marianne wouldn't see me. I felt a relief after they'd gone and no desire to follow them any further. I went into the gallery. One of the artists showing was that German woman Charlotte manages, Karla whatever. I looked at her photos, large black-and-white images of dead children kitschily done up to look as though they were sleeping. I remembered Jarawa's supposed interest in contemporary art and I wondered if by any chance he'd been to Joseph Kimberly and seen any of Marianne's stuff, and if so what he might have thought of it. It was an absurd idea of course, but I couldn't stop myself thinking it.

Afterward I walked to Hyde Park Corner and got the tube to work. I don't know what time it was when I got there but it was getting on, maybe one o'clock. Jo passed me in the corridor without saying a word. I was almost looking forward to getting to my desk as I had this new idea to work on; it had come to me on the tube. What I thought I would do was write a letter to Jarawa. I had no idea whether it would be possible to get it to him of course, but I could work out those details later. I sat down in front of my computer screen, but that was no good so I cleared my desk of all the piles of stuff people had left me and started scribbling thoughts on a sheet of paper. The trouble was that although the idea of writing to Jarawa excited me, I wasn't exactly sure what the point of it was. My writing a letter to him wouldn't make it any more likely that his sentence would be commuted. Perhaps it would give him strength though, knowing that there were those outside, those in foreign countries, who were trying to help him. Then again, whether Jarawa had strength or not would hardly change his fate.

I stared at the sheet of paper for a good while then looked away. There were plenty of other things to do. I still had to get in touch with Jarawa's wife, for example. I'd written her a letter and left several messages on her answering machine, but she had never replied. It was odd, even unpleasant, to be rebuffed like that. The image of the man's hand on Marianne's belly came back to me. Of course, if she'd been trying to get pregnant with her lover I could never forgive her for using condoms with me. I was almost shaking with hate just at the very idea. To try to calm myself down I gazed out the window for a long time. Then eventually Fiona tapped on the door. "Jamie wants to see you."

"Yeah, I'm busy right now."

"He said he wanted to see you as soon as you came in. He said it was urgent."

I went along to Jamie's office. He was talking to someone on the phone and waved at me to sit down. He was saying to whoever it was, I don't give a damn about the cost, I want our name there. Then he put the phone down and stared at me for about a minute without saying a word. It was an old game, the wordless stare. I remembered teachers at school doing it.

Eventually he said, "Okay. Now can you tell me what the hell's going on?"

"What do you mean?"

"You *know* what I fucking mean. . . ."

I didn't reply.

Jamie sighed. "So where do you want me to start? Jo tells me you've become impossible to work with. Fiona says she never knows when you're coming in or where the hell you are. And what the hell's going on with the Jarawa campaign? What was that embassy fiasco all about?"

I remained silent.

"You manage to get a meeting with the ambassador. Great. But then you don't show up for it. Then, from what I gather, you finally get to meet some guy there whose name you can't even remember who shows you some documents. But you can't remember those either. Then you don't show up here until the following afternoon. By that time some of these documents have been released to Reuters and we've missed our opportunity to get in first. Then there's the Freedom Africa protest, which was on channel four news and was reported in the *Guardian* and the *Independent*. So when the triple-murder stuff comes to light, the press go to Freedom Africa for comment and not us. I mean, Jesus Christ. I thought you were supposed to be coordinating this fucking campaign. What the hell's going on?"

"I'm sorry Jamie. I don't know what to say. I've got a few domestic problems."

I'd meant to say personal and not domestic—the term seemed hopelessly old-fashioned—but it had come out like that anyway.

"Domestic problems? Well, let me tell you, when you start screwing everything up 'round here they're not domestic problems, they're my problems!"

Jamie had been almost shouting up until then, but then suddenly he switched and became conciliatory. He started stroking his double chin. "Look. I don't know what's wrong with your life. And I don't want to know, that's your business. I don't want to lose you, because I know you're good and actually we need people like you, people with a solid PR background. People who've worked in the real world." He reached over to a pile of newspapers and magazines. "Do you read the *Economist*?"

"Occasionally."

"Well have you read this?"

He tossed me a month-old copy. Its cover story was about aid agencies and human rights organizations. The library had sent me a photocopy of the article at the time and I'd breezed over it one lunchtime. It predicted a big shake-up in the NGO world— apparently there are too many organizations out there chasing too little money. The drift of the article was that the NGO market was essentially no different from any other and that to survive the shake-up NGOs would have to adopt a more aggressive, market-based approach to their work.

Jamie was saying, "It's why this Freedom Africa thing worries me. I mean, we decided to focus on the Jarawa case in the first place to raise our profile. Now Freedom Africa is trying to muscle in on our game. Even if the campaign fails, in the end I want it to help us. So we have to play it right. Jo's been doing a great job and I was expecting a creative approach from you. Do you understand what I'm saying?"

I said I did. Jamie went on talking. He said there was a plan he'd been mulling over. He had a niece who wanted to come and do volunteer work for us. But he was considering sending her over to Freedom Africa instead, then getting her to report back to us. You mean she'd be some kind of spy, I asked. Jamie frowned. Freedom Africa is supposed to be working hand in hand with us, he replied, but if they don't want to tell us what they're up to I think we're within our rights to try to find out. He talked some more then ended up saying he had to go to a meeting. We both got up. He put his hand on my shoulder. Sort your problems out, he said.

I went back to my office and sat thinking. I looked down at my scribbled ideas for the letter to Jarawa then picked up the sheet of paper and screwed it into a ball. A kind of fear was spreading through me. In a way I didn't care if I lost my job, but I definitely wanted to see the Jarawa campaign through first. Jamie was giving me a chance, I realized. I felt angry at Jo for having complained to him about me. It was a nasty thing to do. She should have come to see me first. Then again, perhaps she actually wanted me out and thought that was the best way to go about it.

I knew I had to sort things out with Marianne. She'd told me she was going down to Montargues at the weekend to see people about the wedding. She was taking Jessica with her. I should seize this opportunity to move out, I thought. I began to work out how to do it. My brother in Tufnell Park could put me up for a while. I don't see him much but he'd let me stay for a week or two. I began to get excited at the prospect. What had seemed so impossible before was to actually confront Marianne. This way I'd be simply presenting her with a fait accompli. More to the point, I'd be presenting myself with a fait accompli. The more I thought about it, the better the idea sounded to me. In the back of my mind somewhere was Christian. He was the example to avoid.

I got home late but Jessica was still up. She was supposed to be having a bath but was running through the house naked. I got hold of her and lifted her up but she started screaming so I put her straight down again. As usual these days I left Marianne to deal with her. Eventually I heard them in the bath giggling and chattering in French together as I watched the news on TV. There was a report on some twenty-year-old kid who was due to be executed in the night by poisonous injection in the state of Florida. For the first time I found myself wondering how exactly Jarawa would be executed if our campaign failed. I was surprised that the question hadn't occurred to me before. I wondered if it would be by guillotine—I remember Christian telling me once that some of the former French colonies in Africa still use the guillotine—and I made a mental note to check up on it at work.

Marianne came back into the lounge and opened some wine. We were talking about the garden or something trivial, but there was an obvious tension in the air. Some guy called Christian rang for you, she was saying, handing me a scrap of paper on which she'd written down his number. I put the number in my Filofax and asked Marianne what date she'd booked the plane tickets for. She was silent for a moment then said, We need to talk. What about, I asked. We were sitting together on the sofa and Marianne moved away from me a little, as if to give herself room to speak. She said she wasn't going down to Montargues after all, at least not just yet, in fact she wasn't so sure we should get married this summer after all. What the hell do you mean, I practically shouted. She scowled at me: For God's sake, keep your voice down! You'll wake up Jessica!

Then Marianne went into a long monologue. She spoke in this artificial manner, slowly, calmly; I could tell she'd rehearsed it. She said that for the past few weeks we hadn't been getting along. She didn't know why; she felt that I resented her. She didn't have any idea why and perhaps I was just taking some other problem of mine out on her. She'd found herself getting angry with me and felt I'd been treating her unfairly. Then there was our sex life. She used to really enjoy making love, but something had gone wrong and it was disturbing her. She said either it seemed like I didn't want to make love anymore, or when I did she could feel some strange violence in me as though if she refused me I'd just go ahead anyway and this had begun to worry her. What did I think?

The dull sound of the television invaded the room. For a brief moment I was ready to tell Marianne everything and then that moment passed. I got up and switched the TV off. In the silence, I could hear Jessica murmuring to herself in her sleep. I sat down and picked up a newspaper. I was shaking a little and in a way that interested me: this business of shaking when I got angry was new.

Well, aren't you going to say anything, said Marianne. No, I replied. It was almost as if I didn't trust myself to speak. I sensed that her little monologue was not over yet. I was scared that she was going to say she wanted to leave me and not give me the opportunity to get in there first. Most of all I was angry that she'd canceled the trip to Montargues. It spoiled my plan to move out, but that wasn't the real reason for my anger. What got to me was that she didn't want to get married anymore. It was a stupid thing to get upset about, given the circumstances, but it hurt me nonetheless. It hurt me deeply.

I pretended to read the newspaper. I didn't want to look up; I didn't want to give her the opportunity to start her monologue again. Eventually she said: Jesus Christ—things can't go on like this. She got up abruptly and went into the bedroom, close to tears. Once she'd gone I put the paper down and breathed out. I stared at a drawing of Jessica's that Marianne had recently pinned to the wall. I hadn't noticed it before. It was of a man. It was a very impressive effort for a three-year-old—the man had huge, menacing black eyes that dominated the picture.

After a few minutes I followed Marianne into the bedroom.

She was taking a shower. The bathroom door was open and I could see her through the frosted glass. I sat down on the bed and watched her—I could see her breasts and curved belly. Ever since I found out about her infidelity she's grown more beautiful. She turned off the shower and slid open the glass doors. Steam poured out.

"Can you pass me a towel?"

I got up and found her a towel. I was suddenly overcome with emotion. I'm sorry, I said, I'm really sorry. She put her wet hand to my face, started stroking my cheek. I started gently rubbing her with the towel, drying her. For a moment or two she seemed to like it, but then she took the towel from me and I realized that she didn't want to make love after all. I went back into the lounge. If I'd stayed and watched her any longer she'd have thought I hadn't understood, but I had.

VIII

I CALLED CHARLOTTE ON THE MOBILE ON MY WAY TO WORK. I ASKED her if she wanted to meet me for lunch, but she said she was busy. What about tomorrow, I said, but she couldn't make that either. Well when can you meet, I asked, shading my eyes with my other hand and steering practically with my elbows. Charlotte said something, but I had the sunroof up and it was hard to hear. Sorry what, I shouted. She said, "I think it's better if we don't see each other anymore. No you don't understand, I replied, I need to see you, it's urgent. I *need* to see you. There was a long pause. Finally she said, Okay, come 'round at twelve-thirty. Don't be late though—I've got an appointment straight after lunch. She sounded pissed off and hung up without saying good-bye.

It was muggy and crowded in the West End. I didn't go straight to work; I sat and had a coffee at one of the cafés in Old

Compton Street. I sat there for half an hour, listening to conversations at other tables and watching people as they walked by. I was wishing I hadn't rung Charlotte. To distract myself I started playing a game—I'd pick out some face from the passersby and try to imagine what would happen to the person in ten, maybe twenty years' time. The trouble was that I kept on coming up with these depressing narratives: the plump girl in the Lycra dress would end up marrying some football bore who abused her . . . the young gay guy would overdose on his thirty-fifth birthday . . . the old woman with the strange hair would die by herself stretched out on the kitchen floor. It was as if this morbidity wasn't so much in me, but all around me, forcing itself on me.

I got up and wandered up Charing Cross Road until I found myself in Bloomsbury. I just didn't feel like going to work. What I decided to do was go to the library in Senate House and check whether they had any of Jarawa's books. I'd never bothered to track them down before. It amazed me now that I hadn't shown the curiosity. There were three books listed in the catalogue. Two of them were political treatises and the third was a volume of poetry. As I went off to dig them out I could feel a disproportionate sense of excitement building up in me. There was that poem I'd read about, the one Jarawa had written about the kid with Down's syndrome. All of a sudden it seemed desperately important that I should read it. Its title, "The Eternal," had stuck in my mind for some reason. I ran my eye down the contents page of the poetry volume but it wasn't there.

The books were a disappointment. The political treatises were written in that convoluted, unreadable Marxist jargon that had been popular in the sixties and no longer meant anything at all. The poetry, on the other hand, sounded dully conventional, like Victorian verse. Perhaps it had been badly translated. I idly flicked through the pages for half an hour or so then gave up. I sat there thinking, trying to analyze my feelings of excitement, then disappointment, and now anger. I wondered why I'd been expecting anything else from his books and why Jarawa seemed so absent from his own writing. There was a picture of him on one of the dust jackets, that by now familiar image of him in the three-piece suit. I tore it out slowly and put it in my wallet next to the photo of Jessica in Marianne's arms, taken just after she'd left the maternity ward. It was the first time I'd ever defaced a library book. It was almost as though I wasn't in control of my actions anymore.

It was too late to go into work by then so I sat reading a magazine for a while then drove over to Charlotte's place in Camden. I pushed the intercom button and she took ages to answer. Finally she buzzed me in and I made my way upstairs, but her door was closed. I knocked and she shouted out: Hang on a minute. I waited there for maybe five minutes or more. I could hear her moving about behind the door. As I waited I could also hear someone coming down the stairs, extremely slowly. Eventually this incredibly old guy rounded the corner. He was taking each step as though for the first time, concentrating all his energies on getting it right, like a toddler. When he got to the landing outside Charlotte's door he looked up and noticed me for the first time. What seemed so extraordinary was that his enormous girth should be held up by such spindly looking legs. Afternoon, I said, but he didn't answer, he just squinted at me with his clear blue eyes, which contrasted so strikingly with the ruin of his face. I recognized him almost immediately, of course: somehow I wasn't at all surprised to see him there outside Charlotte's flat. He was the old man who'd been swimming in the pool the day of Susan Tedeschi's death.

Charlotte opened the door. Her hair was wet; she'd obviously just had a shower. She stood there with her arms folded under her breasts. "It's only twelve. I told you to come 'round at twelve-thirty, for Christ's sake."

She let me in. The flat had changed. It wasn't the tip it had been when I'd last been there—it was much tidier than usual and she'd put up some photographs and paintings on the wall as well.

I said, "Why were you so off with me on the phone?"

"I wasn't off with you."

"Yes you were."

"Okay then, I was." We stood facing each other confrontationally in the middle of the lounge. "You don't ring me for weeks—not that I wanted you to. Then all of a sudden you insist on seeing me. And then you come 'round."

"I wanted to see you again."

"Well you're seeing me. What do you want?"

"Why don't you want me to ring you anymore?"

She sighed. "You'd better sit down."

I sat down. Charlotte sat down beside me. She put her hand on my knee and started talking in an annoying, "patient" tone of voice. "Listen. We had lunch a few times. We slept together a few times. It was nice. If you're feeling insecure about that, well, there's no need. I enjoyed our time together. But at the end of the day you're not my type and I'm not yours. You know that. You knew it from the start—"

"I don't know it. I want to be with you."

"No you don't . . . don't be absurd!" She exhaled sharply through her teeth in exasperation. "What the hell's all this about, anyway?"

I didn't answer. Instead I said, "What attracted you to me that night at the gallery? Why did you seek me out?"

"For God's sake . . . I don't go 'round analyzing every move I make." We stared at each other. "I liked the way you . . . I don't know. But now look at you. You're like . . . I don't know."

"We could be together."

Charlotte started getting really annoyed. "Of course we can't.

What the hell's got into you? We can't be together, not now, not ever. You're already with someone and you've got a kid. Doesn't that mean anything to you?"

"Not anymore."

Charlotte was silent for a moment. Then she started nodding slowly to herself. "Right. I get it now. I get what this ridiculous conversation is about."

"What do you mean?"

"It's pretty obvious. You've found out, haven't you?"

"About what?"

"You know what I'm talking about."

"You mean Marianne and . . ."

"Yes."

I looked away. I put my hand to my Adam's apple and swallowed. Charlotte got up from the sofa, picked up the packet of Silk Cut on the table, lit a cigarette and drew heavily on it. She'd smoked about a third of it before I spoke again. "How did you know? I mean, how did you know?"

She shrugged her shoulders. "I didn't know. I guessed. You get a feeling for these things." She spoke lazily. She took a drag of her cigarette and stared at a blurred photo on the wall. "Or maybe I did know. Maybe I heard some gossip. I can't remember."

"Gossip? You don't even know her."

"I work with artists. Marianne's an artist. You hear things. People talk."

"What were people saying?"

"I told you, I can't remember."

I could feel my heart jolting against my rib cage and the sweat again. What hit home more than anything else was the terrible banality of it all. That was what seemed so grotesque, so humiliating. I noticed I was shaking as well, my left hand in particular. I pressed it against my thigh to try to stop the shaking.

"So you knew all this time. All this time we were sleeping together, you knew Marianne was . . . and you didn't say anything."

"What was there to say? I mean . . . it's not as if *you* were acting like a saint, was it? What the fuck did you think you were doing with *me*, for God's sake?" She came and sat down beside me again. Her tone softened a little. "I'm sorry. But you're the one who wanted to come 'round."

She put her hand on my knee again. I put my hand on her shoulder then moved it down to her breast. I could feel her tensing up, ever so slightly. We sat like that for a while then I turned to kiss her.

"No, wait a second. If you've come here because you want to prove something, then you'd better leave right now. Your problems with Marianne have got nothing to do with me."

I tried to kiss her again. She pushed me away in irritation like a mother with an importunate child. "No, leave me alone!" She took my hand off her breast and I put it 'round her waist. Suddenly she sprang up from the sofa. "Jesus Christ!" She stood over me, hands on her hips. "Okay then. So you want to fuck me, then fuck me. I don't think you could even get it up in the state you're in. Could you?"

She pulled her dress over her shoulders, threw it on the sofa beside me. She had a bra on but no slip. Her sudden nakedness shocked me. It seemed almost brutal, like a weapon to be used against me. She came toward me. I sat there doing nothing, not even looking at her. She started unbuckling my belt.

"Could you?"

She was crouched down between my legs, maybe kneeling. She had my belt unbuckled and now she was unbuttoning my fly. I shoved at her shoulders. I shoved her much harder than I'd meant to and she fell to the ground. There was a clumsy thump as she landed. She lay there not moving, staring up at me. "Just get out of here," she said finally. "Get the hell out."

I almost fell down the stairs. I was shaking all over, I felt strange. Then as I was walking down Charlotte's street I felt something on my face and I put my hand to my cheek. It was wet. I was crying. It shocked me. An old lady was looking at me with ill-disguised curiosity. I needed to sit down somewhere, but obviously I couldn't go into a pub or café, so I ended up walking by the canal, then sitting down on a bench overlooking it. I gazed into the stagnant water. It was covered with a kind of oily scum that made rainbow patterns in the sun. A disintegrating milk carton bobbed along and farther down I could see the swollen body and filthy fur of some animal swirling gracefully in the eddy. I took deep regular breaths to control my heartbeat and stop the shaking. After a while, a quarter of an hour maybe, I could feel a kind of calm descend over me and a resolution building up. It was clear what I had to do.

It wasn't easy driving; I couldn't get rid of my shake. I had to really concentrate on the road ahead and at one point I almost collided with some other guy. It scared the hell out of me. I had to pull over for a moment to steady my nerves. I felt like having a joint or something to take the edge off things but in the end I didn't do anything about it. I just couldn't be bothered to go through the whole sordid hassle of scoring.

Finally I got to Holland Road. There was a parking space right outside the block of flats, but somehow that seemed too obvious and it took me ages to find another one, way up the road toward Shepherd's Bush. I walked back slowly. There was a row of buzzers by the front door, but only one with no name against it—I pressed it. A man answered. "Yes?"

"Is Marianne there?"

"Who is this, please?"

"I need to speak to you."

"Who am I talking to, please?"

"I live with Marianne."

There was a long pause. "You'd better come up. Third floor."

There was a lift, but I walked up the stairs anyway. The building, which looked dingy from the road, was elegantly maintained inside, with paintings on the wall and a hint of thirties-style luxury. It can't be cheap to rent here, I thought to myself, and I could feel something quite terrible inside me, a sort of tearing hate.

The man was peering at me through a chained door. "Don't worry," I said, "I'm not going to do anything to you." He unchained the door and opened up. "I suppose I've been expecting you for some time now. Come in." I wondered what exactly he meant by that. He was wearing an expensive-looking dressing gown, possibly silk. A gift from Marianne, perhaps.

I went in and glanced briefly about the bedsit. It was reasonably spacious but spartan in its decoration. There was a double bed and chest of drawers at one end of the room; at the other, a tiny kitchen and dinner table by the window. Between the two was a hearth. On the mantelpiece above sat a glass vase with a simple bouquet of flowers and a photo of Marianne grinning wildly at the camera. Behind the vase and photo was a huge mirror. A skirt that I recognized as Marianne's hung over the back of a chair.

"Is Marianne here?"

"No."

I stood there not moving, accusing him with my stare.

"You don't believe me, do you? Go and look in the bathroom if you like."

His voice was crisp, patrician. I kicked gently at the door that led to the bathroom; it creaked open and I peered inside. There was no one there. I shouldn't have done that, I thought, I shouldn't have kicked at the door. I've made myself look foolish.

"Please, sit down," the man said, removing Marianne's skirt from the chair, folding it neatly, holding it in one hand and patting it with the other. "You'll have to excuse me for a moment. I'll get dressed. Then we'll talk." He went to the chest of drawers, pulled a drawer out to put Marianne's skirt away, opened another and took out some of his own clothes. "Please excuse me."

He went into the bathroom and I was by myself again. What struck me was the man's civility, his politeness. It was so strange being here inside the flat when I'd spent so many mornings outside on the pavement looking in. There was something about the simplicity of the room that wrenched at me. It had the innocence of a bedsit that student lovers might share. From the bathroom I could hear the man splashing in the basin. What was he doing in his dressing gown at this time of day, it suddenly occurred to me. I looked over to the bed—it hadn't been properly made. The cover had been thrown over it in an approximate fashion. He wasn't waiting for Marianne, I realized. She'd already been and gone.

Music wafted through the room: it had been on low and I was so keyed up that I hadn't even noticed it before. It was Mozart. I knew the piece for once. It was one of Marianne's favorites. I remembered when I'd first heard it. It was maybe the fourth or fifth time we'd made love. We'd laid the duvet down on the floor of Marianne's old flat in Menilmontant and she'd put the music on and then we'd made love on the floor. It churned me up inside thinking about it.

The man came back. He'd combed his thin hair into place and was now wearing corduroy trousers and an ironed white shirt.

"I'm afraid I don't know your name."

"My name?" For some reason I hadn't expected that question. "Bourne. Matthew Bourne."

The man looked surprised. "Actually I think we already know each other. . . . I mean, we've spoken on the phone."

"I don't think so."

"Perhaps I've made a mistake. You don't work for a human rights organization, do you?"

"Yes, I do."

"Wasn't it you who contacted me over the Jarawa business?"

"I . . . Yes, it must have been me."

He extended his hand. "Richard Weldon. Professor Weldon. You wanted me to sign a letter of protest."

"Yes. I remember now."

He rubbed his badly shaven chin. "In fact, I'd been meaning to write to you. I felt bad about refusing and I don't think I properly argued my case over the phone. It was more the *kind* of letter you wanted me to sign that I was worried about than the idea in general. It just struck me as naïve and very open to criticism. What I'd have liked to do is set up a meeting between you and Pierre Douff, I don't know if you've heard of him—"

"No."

"Well, he did a lot of work on West Africa in the eighties. I believe there are some very serious doubts regarding some of Jarawa's political activities. I mean, human rights abuses—"

I broke in. "I don't believe that. I really don't. I mean, I'm in charge of this campaign and I've looked very carefully into . . . I mean, there're a lot of people who have vested interests . . . I mean . . . what does it matter anyway. What does it matter what he's done. Does that mean we should work less hard for his release . . . are you actually saying you think he should be killed?"

I'd suddenly got all excited, my words were falling over each other almost incomprehensibly and I wasn't expressing myself well. I couldn't get rid of my damned shake either. The man looked disconcerted. "No of course not . . . but perhaps now is not the moment to discuss this."

"No."

There was an awful silence. I wiped the sweat from my forehead with the back of my hand and looked out the window. Two lovers were arguing on a street corner.

Finally the man said, "What did you want to talk to me about?"

I laughed, I don't know why, and it sounded sinister. I said: "How long have you and Marianne been seeing each other?"

The man didn't reply immediately, then he spoke slowly, with deliberation. "Look, I don't think I feel at liberty to say anything more than what Marianne has already told you."

"But she hasn't told me anything, don't you see?"

"No. I don't see. You mean she hasn't told you of her decision?"

"What decision?"

"You don't know?"

"Know what? I don't know anything."

"I see. I see." I was shaking badly, sweating too. The man stood up. "Listen. I think it's not me you need to talk to, it's Marianne. I think you should try to calm down then go home and see her. Don't you think that would be best?"

"Yes. You're right. I'm sorry, I . . ."

He waved his hand. "I'm the one who should be apologizing. Please believe me, I'm sorry it's come to this. I'm honestly very sorry."

From anyone else it would have sounded incredibly insincere but somehow I believed him. He reached into his pocket and took out a packet of cigarettes, a French brand.

"Do you smoke?"

"No."

He lit a cigarette; the acrid aroma smelled vaguely familiar. Of course: I'd smelled it on Marianne. It reminded me of being in bed with her . . .

"Perhaps a drink then?"

"Okay. A whisky. If you've got any."

"Sure."

There was a kind of built-in sideboard that divided the kitchen area from the rest of the room. A few bottles were lined up there by the wall.

"Ice? Soda?"

He was holding one of those soda bottles with a pressure trigger on the top. It looked like some strange sort of weapon.

"No, straight."

He turned his back to me as he started preparing the drinks. It hurt me that the man hadn't known my name or what I did. It meant that Marianne never spoke to him about me, that I hadn't been worth the conversation. I wondered why he smoked French cigarettes, too. It was a kind of pretension, when he didn't actually seem the pretentious sort, despite the silk dressing gown. Of course, if he'd picked up the habit while living in France, it wouldn't be pretentious at all, merely normal. The thought entered me like a twisting knife. Perhaps he and Marianne had met up in France and not here, perhaps they'd been together since before Marianne and I had even known each other. It would explain a lot of things. How was it, for example, that she'd spoken such excellent English when I'd first met her, when she'd never lived in an English-speaking country? My mind scrolled wildly through scenario after scenario: perhaps the man has a sick wife he can't leave . . . perhaps he has children he doesn't want to abandon . . . then again what exactly was Marianne's "decision"?

As he fixed the drinks, the man kept talking. "You may be interested to know that I actually met Jarawa once. At a conference. Must have been some time in the mid-eighties. It was while he was, briefly, minister of culture. He's got a lot of charm, I have to admit . . . he knows a hell of a lot about the arts as well."

The man left his cigarettes and lighter on the sideboard. I recognized the Zippo lighter at once: it was mine. Marianne had given it to me years ago to replace one that had once belonged to my grandfather. I'd lost my "heirloom" in a pub and had been mildly upset about it at the time. When I'd come home the next day Marianne had given me the Zippo and put her arms around me. Later on, when we'd both given up smoking cigarettes on account of Jessica, I'd mislaid it. Only I hadn't mislaid it after all. Marianne had taken it back and given it to her lover. I couldn't believe she'd done that. I just couldn't believe it. But the evidence was right there before my eyes.

I began to feel horribly dizzy. The man was talking. It was like a dream. I couldn't hear what he was saying, only the Mozart that was on low, that was reaching its civilized crescendo. Then the dizziness passed and an extraordinary lightness and clarity seemed to possess me. The sun was spilling in through the window, splashing over the room, reflecting off the bottles and dazzling me. The man's back seemed obscure, a dark rock looming over me. I could feel the sweat trickling down my forehead as I got up from the chair, picked up the vase from the mantelpiece, and brought it crashing down on the man's head. Suddenly, the air exploded in a spectacular shower of water and glass shards, shimmering in the sunlight, falling slowly like fireworks, like snowflakes, to the floor. I remembered the snow dome my great aunt had given me as a boy, with Saint Bernadette praying in the grotto. She'd brought it back from Lourdes. I'd found the snow dome so beautiful that I'd shaken it and shaken it again and again until finally it broke. Now I felt I was inside it, drowning.

The man fell soundlessly. For a moment I just stood there,

transfixed, watching him. He lay on his back, not moving at all. Then he started gesturing to me, ever so feebly. I knelt down, put my ear to his mouth. I could hear him murmuring something but I couldn't make out what—after a while the murmuring stopped, but his lips continued to move. I sat up a little and looked into his open eyes. He was smiling at me, a beatific smile that absurdly reminded me of Jessica's grinning teddy bear. I stared back. I stayed there crouched over him for a while, maybe a minute, maybe five minutes, before I realized that he was dead. He'd died as he smiled at me. I hadn't noticed it, not at first. His eyes still engaged with mine somehow and I found it difficult to pull away. But I did, in the end.

I slumped back down in the chair by the dinner table, assuming the same position I'd been in only moments before as the man had been telling me about Jarawa, his back turned toward me. I visualized him there by the sideboard and almost immediately I began to relive it all again, for the first time, as though I couldn't stop myself vomiting up something I'd just eaten. I saw myself rise from the chair, grab the vase—how had I done that with my shaking hands?—and bring it down on the man's head . . . then the fine shower of glass and water. . . . The strange thing was that I saw it all not from my own perspective but from some neutral position, facing both myself and the man. I was looking into my own eyes. . . . It was only much later that I realized what had happened, that as I'd picked up the vase I'd in fact been staring into the mirror above the mantelpiece, staring at myself, at the man, at everything, as though I weren't really a part of it, as though I were the voyeur once again and for the last time.

My glass of whisky was still sitting there on the sideboard, just as the man had left it. I drank it down, then poured myself another one and drank that down as well. As I poured, I noticed a strange thing: my shaking had gone. I looked out the window. The lovers were still there, still arguing. How could they be? It was like some relic from the distant past. I picked up the man's cigarettes and took one from the packet. I lit it and inhaled deeply, feeling a rush of dizziness so overpowering that I had to sit back down again. It had been such a long time since I'd smoked pure tobacco that I was quite unused to it.

Everything moved in dream colors, deep blues, greens. I felt quite helpless, I could hardly move. I thought how nice it would be to go to sleep and contemplated lying down on the bed, Marianne and the man's bed, then decided against it. There was a phone. I hadn't noticed it before, it was sitting on the floor in the corner. It was one of those old black ones with a proper dialing face. I picked up the receiver to call the police. With astonishment I realized I didn't know or had forgotten the emergency number. Was it 999, or 000, or 123, or something else? I sat there holding the receiver for a long, long time. Then eventually I put it down again.

I looked at the man. There were no visible signs of violence on his body, but a thick halo of blood welled out from behind his head like in an Italian painting. Scattered all about were glass, water, and the fresh flowers, tulips. Some were beside the body and some draped over it, as if for a mysterious funeral ritual. As the pool of blood slowly grew it mingled with the water, creating little rivulets that marred the perfection of the halo. It wasn't possible that he was dead, I said to myself. A single blow from a glass vase could hardly have killed him, not so quickly at any rate. People have fallen through plate-glass windows without sustaining fatal injuries. I looked into his eyes again. They were dead eyes. I'd already seen eyes like that when I'd identified Susan Tedeschi's body.

I thought about that day in Oxford, I could remember it so well, better than anything else, so much better than what had happened only a few minutes ago. I remembered everything Christian had said to me and everything I had said to him. I'd stared at Susan Tedeschi's face when I shouldn't have. Had my fingertips accidentally grazed her body? Had I suppressed a desire to touch it? The debilitating fear and anger I had felt toward Christian was quite misplaced, I realized. It had been his wife's fault, not his.

I reached into my jacket pocket and pulled out my Filofax. Tucked in the back was the scrap of paper Marianne had given me the other night with Christian's number on it. It was an 0207 number. He must have moved up to London, or maybe he was just staying with friends. I dialed. I said, "It's me. You called the other day."

"Yes."

"Something's happened."

"What?"

"I can't tell you over the phone."

"I'll meet you somewhere. Where are you?"

I gave him the address and hung up.

IX

I WAITED. IT WAS A HUGE EFFORT TO DO ANYTHING. THE MAN seemed to have grown in death; his body shrank the room. I thought of getting up and closing his eyes or something, but in the end I just concentrated on not looking at the body. It was its utter stillness that was so intolerable, that gave him this Olympian air of authority, as though he were in deep contemplation and ready to crush my tiny concerns at any moment. The silence was oppressive as well. I would have liked to have put the Mozart CD back on again but I didn't have the energy for it. Then it occurred to me that, in any case, I'd destroyed that piece of music forever. For the rest of my life, whenever I heard it I would no longer be reminded of Marianne's young body, instead I would remember the one now stretched out before me. I would see not Marianne's smile but her lover's. The idea tore at

me and I just sat there hypnotized with shock, not doing anything, not thinking anything.

Suddenly the intercom buzzed. My head felt light and my
legs heavy as though I'd been sitting down for hours. I looked
around for the intercom; it was by the door. I had to step over
the body to get to it. Christian's voice crackled over the little
speaker, then I buzzed him in. I stood by the door. I could hear
him climbing the stairs, two or three at a time. I wondered why
he hadn't taken the lift. Then I could feel him behind the door.

I opened it slightly. "No, you can't come in."

Christian was breathless from the stairs. "What the hell's—"

"You'd better go. I don't know why I rang you."

"What's happened?"

"Please, just go."

Christian forced his way past me. It took me by surprise and I
made no attempt to stop him. It was as if I had no strength left in
me at all. He stopped when he saw the body, though. He just
stared down in horrified astonishment. "Oh my God . . . oh
Jesus."

I stood there looking at Christian looking at the body. An
overwhelming feeling of childlike guilt swept through me and
all I could think was how badly I'd let him down. "I'm sorry, I'm
really sorry." The memory came back to me of that day at the
hospital and the nurse explaining to me how Christian's wife
had died and how I'd suppressed the desire to say: "It wasn't me
who killed her."

"I think I'm going to be sick. I'm going to be sick."

Christian rushed to the window, almost tripping over the
body, and hung his head outside for a minute or so. He wasn't
sick though. Eventually he sat down on the chair, the one I'd
been sitting on, the one I'd got up from to grab the vase from
the mantelpiece. He looked quite stunned. I said I was sorry
again but he didn't reply, not at first. He just sat there staring, his

gangly body all folded up like an anglepoise lamp. Eventually he asked who the man was, but I said nothing. There was another longish moment of silence.

"Have you called the police?"

"I haven't called anyone except you."

"But who is he?"

I still didn't answer.

"Do you want me to ring the police?"

"Yes . . . no . . . I don't know . . ."

The dull warmth of the summer afternoon had invaded me and the muffled cries of kids playing cricket in the street seemed almost more interesting than my conversation with Christian. But that must have been when I told him I wanted to get the body out of there. I hadn't even realized it was what I wanted to do until I'd put the desire into words. I must have said something like: I don't want Marianne to find her lover like this. All dead and bloody. I owe her that at least. I begged him to help me and he told me to sit down. He didn't speak for a long, long time after that. He sat down himself, but turned away from me, his arms and legs continually shifting about like an upturned beetle's. A tap was dripping in the bathroom. The man couldn't have turned it off properly. These vestiges of his last actions were peculiar, as though bits of him had yet to die.

Finally Christian said, "You're going to have to stay here, I'll be back in twenty minutes."

"What are you going to do?"

"Nothing. I'll be back in twenty minutes."

"Okay."

I let him go. I didn't want to be left alone with the body again but it was a relief that Christian was doing something, taking the situation in hand. An absurd gratitude toward him swept through me. I didn't really care too much about what exactly he was up to. Perhaps he was calling the police. I sat in a kind of trance

smoking cigarette after cigarette. The sun had fallen a little lower
in the sky and the body now cast a shadow over the opposite wall
and the bed. It meant that practically wherever I looked I saw
either the body or its shadow.

My mind flickered uncertainly from one half-formed idea to
another. I recalled my grandmother once telling me about the
death of *her* grandmother, how the family had sat up in vigil over
the body the night she'd died, and how my grandmother hadn't
wanted to at all, but her mother had made her. For the first time
I imagined my grandmother as a young girl, a frightened, trau-
matized girl shut up in a stuffy Edwardian room with a dead relative. I suddenly felt a great flow of sympathy toward her and I
could remember her face as she'd told me that story: it was so
clear and I could read the pain in it. How was it that I hadn't
seen it before? And yet it was strange how my visual imagination
seemed so much sharper, more real to me now. For instance,
when I thought about Jarawa it was no longer as some kind of
blank icon. It was as though the death of this other man had
woken him up for me.

Christian came back in as I was stubbing out the last of the
man's cigarettes. It seemed he'd been away only an instant, but
judging from the number of cigarette butts in the ashtray, he
must have been gone a good forty minutes. He had a whole lot
of stuff with him that he'd brought up in the lift: cleaning prod-
ucts, trash bags, a bucket, a white sheet, a large tarpaulin-like
cover . . . "Where did you get all this from," I asked. He said from
a home improvement center up in Shepherd's Bush.

After he'd got everything into the room and shut the door he
unfolded the sheet and placed it beside the body. "Here, help me
roll him onto it." I stepped onto the other end of the sheet, by
the man's feet. The body wasn't easy to roll though. In the end
we kind of dragged it to the middle of the sheet, which Christian folded on top of it. But the sheet got caught on the man's

lower lip, pulling it down to expose his teeth, turning his smile into a sneer. Christian disentangled the sheet from the man's lip and pulled it back from his face. A pool of blood—congealed and slightly lumpy, like poorly made gravy—had formed where the man's head had rested on the ground.

Christian spread the tarpaulin over the floor and we lifted the now-shrouded body onto it. The top end of the sheet had already started to stain red, but the tarpaulin looked plastic and waterproof. Around the edges were reinforced holes through which was threaded a bright orange nylon rope. Immediately I grasped what Christian was trying to do. He was going to pull the rope tight to make a kind of bag out of the tarpaulin, with the body inside. I stood by and watched as he pushed the man's knees into his chest so the body would fit properly on the tarpaulin. His knees kept springing back gently, but somehow Christian eventually maneuvered the body so it was curled up and ball-like. I stared down. The body's fetal position and the fact that it lay shrouded in white reminded me of the ultrasound images I'd seen of Jessica before she'd been born, when I'd gone to the prenatal clinic with Marianne.

We lifted up the tarpaulin around the body and Christian pulled the nylon rope tight and knotted it. Then he got out some industrial tape he'd bought and started taping up the bag to secure it properly. When he'd finished, there was this huge thing sitting in the middle of the floor. It didn't look like a body now. It didn't look like anything at all.

"My car's right outside the building. He won't fit in the boot but I've already put the backseat down."

We half pushed, half pulled the body along the floor, out through the door and into the lift then outside onto the pavement. A few kids—maybe the ones who I'd heard playing street cricket—looked on as we tried to haul the body into the car over the folded-down seat at the back. I could see the two lovers on the corner as well. They were still there, which seemed odd. There would be hundreds of witnesses of course. But I didn't care.

The trouble was our hands kept slipping on the plastic tarpaulin and it took a few minutes before we got the body in the car. It finally slid in and bounced about a little like a giant football. Christian slammed the car door. "Let's get back and clean up." It was warm and the desire to be somewhere quite different—perhaps the swimming pool—was strong in me. I followed Christian back inside without saying a word.

Putting on the rubber gloves he'd brought with him, Christian went to the bathroom, filled up the bucket then started working on the pool of blood. I looked out the window. There was a tree on the street corner not too far from the window and while Christian cleaned I watched it rustling in the breeze, not thinking of anything, except perhaps of the melancholy beauty of the tree. Eventually I turned back to the room. The soap suds in the bucket were pink now but all trace of blood on the floor had gone. Christian was sitting back, rolling himself a cigarette. "Of course, it won't escape any real investigation. If the cops come 'round and examine the place I mean."

"It doesn't matter."

The trouble was, the floor tiles Christian had cleaned the blood from were now a slightly different color from the rest. They were shiny and stood out. I said this to Christian and he squinted down at the floor. "I could clean all the tiles. Then they'd all be the same."

"No. Marianne would notice."

In the end what Christian did was stamp around the place where the blood had been, trying to rub in some of the dirt from his shoes. That took some of the shine off it—if you weren't actually looking for anything you probably wouldn't have noticed the difference. After that Christian started sweeping up the glass and flowers while I tidied, washing out the bucket, chucking stuff into the trash bags he'd bought. I put the whisky bottle back in its proper place, washed up the whisky glasses and wiped down everything I could remember touching. It was a futile exercise of course. As Christian had already pointed out, if the police actually came 'round here they'd obviously find evidence of one sort or another. They'd find a hair, a footprint, or maybe blood between the cracks in the tiles. . . . All that was a question of time and a matter of complete indifference to me.

As all the cleaning was going on I'd slipped into a kind of reverie. I'd almost forgotten what had happened until the phone rang. It was incredibly loud. I froze and so did Christian. The phone rang and rang, six times, ten times. When eventually it stopped I said, Okay, we've got to get out of here. I started to panic and gabble, losing control. Christian said hang on, there's no point in hurrying this, messing it up, whoever rang is not going to come 'round right now. I'm not so sure, I replied. My left hand had started shaking again and I was stuttering and rushing over my words. Christian said no, slow down, just sit down, we've got to do this properly. I sat down, relieved once more to have him tell me what to do. Christian began gathering up all the cleaning things and putting them into one of the trash bags. Then he piled everything by the door. After that he went into the bathroom for a moment. When he came out again he said, "Is everything in place here? I mean, is this the way you want to leave the room?"

I looked around for the last time. The room seemed curiously empty without the body. I looked over to the partially made bed. I picked up the lighter, my lighter, and put it in my pocket. "Yes," I said. But as soon as we'd left the room and Christian had shut the door behind us I remembered something. I'd forgotten

Marianne's skirt. It had been hanging on the back of the chair and the man had put it away so that I could sit down. I should have got the skirt out again. It didn't matter really. It's hard to explain, but somehow it made me feel incredibly sad that I'd forgotten to put the skirt back on the chair.

It was hot in the car. I could smell blood—or perhaps it was just my imagination—and I wound down the window. We didn't talk. I didn't ask Christian where we were going, but then we were on the Hammersmith flyover. For quite a while I couldn't rid myself of that feeling of panic that had been triggered by the phone ringing. I wished I'd picked up the phone and found out who'd been calling. I was certain it had been Marianne. Perhaps she was heading over there right now. She would be surprised to find that the man wasn't at the bedsit. Would she notice anything different? Would she notice the shiny patch on the checkered tiles? Perhaps not. There would be the missing vase of course. I'd forgotten about that. Its disappearance would seem mysterious, very mysterious. I couldn't imagine how Marianne would explain it to herself.

I watched Christian as he drove—he hardly moved at all. I'd always looked down on men who were happy to cede control to another man, perhaps it was one of the reasons why Christian had rubbed me up the wrong way at times. Now it seemed I'd become the very thing I despised. We passed a field of cows, then another, speeding past them so fast that they appeared to be the merest blur of biology. There was something curiously comforting about being in a car accelerating through the countryside: it was to do with the fact that the motorway was a kind of nonplace. In the world but not of it.

Christian cut through my reflections. "It was a shock. Seeing the body. I mean I've never seen a dead body before."

"I have."

He didn't say anything further. He looked like he was thinking, or maybe he was just concentrating on driving. I glanced at my watch: it was two-thirty. An instant later I looked at it again and it was three. Suddenly Christian slowed down. It was the Oxford turnoff, which crossed back over the motorway via a little bridge. As he swung the car around I could feel the body rolling about a little in the back.

We were now on a suburban road on the outskirts of town and after the otherworldliness of the bedsit and the motorway it was odd to see people going about their normal business. I noticed a young woman with a shopping bag walking down the street with her daughter, aged five or six. The girl was skipping along behind, one foot in the gutter, the other on the footpath, talking or singing to herself.

We stopped outside a semidetached house in Headington with a For Sale sign out front. Christian got out of the car. "Wait here a minute." He hadn't told me what his plans were and I hadn't asked. There was almost this feeling that somehow I was already out of the picture. In some respects I had yet to even leave the bedsit and I saw myself kneeling over the man, desperately trying to catch his final words.

I could hear Christian putting things in the boot. Then he got back into the driving seat. He'd changed his shirt. He'd washed his face too, wetting his hair and slicking it back. It had been cut. I hadn't noticed that before. He had new glasses as well. He'd lost his hippie look and it changed him, in some way making him look older and more purposeful.

Christian was driving again. We passed through suburbs into a kind of transitional zone, not town, not country. There were abandoned buildings, warehouses or old factories maybe, and tarmac areas with great cracks and grass and weeds pushing up through them. It was empty with the strange exception of a few girls hanging about. They were of an indeterminate age. Then finally we emerged into the countryside.

We didn't drive for long though. We turned off into a country lane then into a dirt track darkened with overhanging trees. It was a small forest or something. We bumped along for a while then at one point Christian stopped abruptly, pulled over to one side. "It's here, I think." He got out, went 'round to my side, and opened my door. At first I didn't move and Christian didn't say anything. He turned away and got some tools and this camp bed thing out of the boot and unfolded it, then just stood there and rolled a cigarette. He seemed deep in thought. Eventually I got out. Christian said, "Okay. We've got to get him out of the back. It'll soon be over." I noticed how Christian said "him" and not "it" when he talked about the body. I said, "Okay."

It was very hot. I grabbed hold of the nylon rope around the tarpaulin and pulled the body to the edge of the seat, then Christian eased it onto the ground. "I'm going to take all this tape crap off then take him out and lay him on the stretcher. He'll be easier to carry like that." He got some secateurs from the boot and started hacking through the tape, then he undid the rope. The tarpaulin fell away. The body was on its side, still curled up in fetal position. Even like that, even shrouded in a sheet, he was somehow recognizable. It was the shape of his body. The top half of the sheet was stained red with blood now, stiff with it, as though that part was another piece of material altogether. It looked like a hood for a condemned man.

Christian grappled with the body, but it wouldn't uncurl. maybe rigor mortis had set in. In the end we hauled it onto the camp bed just as it was. Lying there on its side it looked like a solitary child coiled up against the cold. As long as his body was there, as long as his distinctive shape was still recognizable it seemed there was still a breath of life about the man.

We positioned ourselves on either end of the camp bed and picked it up. Right at that moment though I heard the sound of a car from up the road. Christian stayed calm. "We'll carry him behind the car then throw the tarpaulin over him." I could hardly hold my end of the bed I was shaking so much, but Christian stared at me ferociously. "It'll be all right. Just do what I say." We got the body and camp bed behind the car and then stood about while the car passed. It was a man driving, tweed cap, Barbour, a caricature of a country type. The man slowed down slightly and peered at us with hostile curiosity, but Christian waved and he drove on and disappeared 'round the bend.

I grabbed Christian by the shoulder. "God . . . we look so bloody suspicious. What's he going to think? We've got to get out of here. What's he going to think?"

"He's not going to think anything. He's going to think we came here to walk in the forest."

"I can't take it. . . . Do you understand? Do you?"

I was shaking really badly. Christian got out his tobacco and Rizlas again. He was talking very slowly, evenly. "I'm going to roll a cigarette, and I'm going to put a bit of dope in. Then we'll smoke it, it'll take the edge off things. Then we'll be calmer. We'll be able to go through with this thing and then it'll be over. Okay?"

"Okay."

Suddenly I felt all compliant again. Christian rolled the cigarette and lit it, then handed it to me and we smoked it together. It was true, I felt calmer afterward. I felt in a daze too. There was a gate near the car that led into an unkempt path through the forest. Christian unlatched the gate and we carried the camp bed through, with the curled body and the tarpaulin over it, and laid the whole lot down again while Christian closed the gate.

I said, "People will see the car there, though."

"So what?"

We picked the camp bed up again and made our way into the forest. It was dark, the trees closing over our heads, engulfing us. Twigs and leaves crackled underfoot. In the silence it seemed shockingly loud. We trudged on for maybe ten or fifteen minutes and every so often we stopped and put the camp bed down. Christian didn't seem entirely sure where he was going. I said, what if we bump into someone? Christian said, we won't. It's a weekday. Nobody ever comes down here anyway.

The dazed feeling came and went. I remembered the whiskies I'd had at the bedsit. I was confused as to whether I'd had them before or after the event. If it was after, I'd risked swallowing some of the glass shards that had showered the room. Maybe the shards were already inside me, worming their way into my stomach lining. Maybe I was about to die a horribly painful death. But I didn't care. A big black bird swooped down at us, then swooped back up to the canopy and beyond. I was sweating profusely.

"It's down here."

We turned off the path and made our way through the trees and undergrowth, it wasn't easy. We were moving down into a little depression, the ground was thick with moldering leaves which were springy underfoot and gave you the impression you were walking over a mattress. Then at the bottom of the depression there was a kind of rocky bit that rose steeply up on the other side. Between two rocks was an entrance to a cave, as tall as a doorway and a little narrower. A metal frame and a barred gate had been fitted into the entrance, as if for a prison cell. It was padlocked but the padlock was rusted up and obviously hadn't been opened in years. Christian got a hammer out of his pocket and knocked the padlock off on the first hit. "It's through here."

We got the body off the camp bed and pushed it through the gate. We were in the narrow, vaulted gallery of a cave, a corridor that led nowhere. I noticed some wire mesh covering a hole in the cave floor. Christian was already on his knees prising off the wire mesh, which was pinned firmly to the rock with what looked like giant staples. He was taking out the staples with a pincer-like tool he'd brought along with him. In the meantime I was crouched down on the ground, which was dusty and covered in dried droppings, maybe bat droppings. Then I noticed a little plaque cemented to the bottom of the cave wall:

†

In memory of
JOHN FRIEDMAN
1961–1970

Much loved and missed by
his mother, father and sister

Christian had got the wire mesh off. We pushed the curled-up body to the hole. For a moment it was balanced there, teetering on the edge like a giant golf ball, stiff with rigor mortis. Then the body keeled over into the darkness below. I heard it roll down, bump on a ridge or something, then silence for a good second until a dull thump and maybe a distant splash. It must have been a good long way down. I stared into the hole but I couldn't see anything, just the blackness. I felt a stale coolness on my face and I shivered and stood back, then I went out of the cave.

Outside the sun's rays strained through the trees and the air smelled warm and alive. I sat down on the ground by the camp bed waiting for Christian to come out, but he was quite awhile. I could hear hammering noises from inside. There was a huge rock leaning by the side of the cave; it looked like a flattened sphere. It looked as though it would have fitted snugly over the entrance and I wondered if that was where it had been originally. Perhaps it had broken off and rolled away thousands of years ago in an earthquake.

Eventually Christian came back out. His jeans were dirty at the knees and he looked blank and exhausted as he closed the gate and put the broken padlock back on. "Finished. Let's go."

His voice sounded mechanical. I was standing now by one end of the camp bed and Christian walked over to the other end. "I don't want this thing anymore. I don't want to see it again. Let's dump it over there." Then he changed his mind. "No, we'd better take it back after all."

We walked the bed back to the car. It seemed to take much less time to get back out of the forest than to get in. There was the darkness then suddenly we came to the edge of the forest and the gate, the sun overpowering my eyes. I sat down by the edge of the path, overcome with fatigue. I looked at my watch and it said three. That didn't seem unlikely but then I noticed that the second hand wasn't moving. I shook it but that didn't make any difference, the watch had stopped. I'd only recently put a new battery in.

Christian was folding up the camp bed and then I could hear the sound of a car coming from up the road. It was the man in the tweed cap, coming back from the other direction—I almost knew it was him before I looked up. This time he slowed right down and stared at us carefully, first me then Christian, as if he were trying to commit our faces to memory for future reference. For a moment I thought he was going to stop, but he didn't. He suddenly accelerated and was gone. Christian said, "Okay, get in."

We drove into Oxford, into the center—I hadn't been there since that time with Christian. He parked the car somewhere off George Street and we got out. For a while we just walked around aimlessly. It was like we were sleepwalking. I could see that Christian was even more tired than I was, there were dark lines around his eyes and mouth that hadn't been there before.

There were no students about. They'd probably all gone home for the holidays. The Cornmarket was full of people though, locals, you could hear from the accent. There was a sprinkling of Japanese and American tourists as well. We walked right down to the Botanical Gardens then across the meadows behind Magdalen College. Eventually we cut back through to Broad Street. We were walking about for an hour or so, maybe an hour and a half even. We didn't say a word to each other, not until later when we got to the pub by Blackwell's. In the meadows the sun was low in the sky, splashing a creamy light over a herd of deer grazing in the distance. We stopped a moment to gaze at the deer then looked into each other's expressionless faces. I could feel myself relaxing slightly for the first time that day, maybe for the first time in weeks. It was this sense of giving in to whatever was in store for me. It was the dying sun and this dazed, silent intimacy. Christian put his hand on my shoulder then we turned 'round to walk back.

The pub was one of those low-beamed affairs with a real log fire, only it wasn't lit now of course, since it was summer. All about us we could hear low, satisfied fragments of conversation as we watched each other over our drinks. Finally I broke the silence. I asked Christian how he'd known about the cave in the forest. It was the first time either of us had spoken since the car and my voice sounded utterly unlike my own. Christian didn't answer straightaway, he just sat drinking his pint. But then eventually he gave me the story. He said he'd lived near the forest as a child, but it had been much bigger then—they'd cleared a lot of it since, for farming land. There'd been an accident in the cave a long time ago. A couple of kids had been playing in the forest one day. They'd found the cave and one of them had slipped and fallen down the hole. Some firemen had gone down the hole but they hadn't been able to find the missing boy. In the end they had to send in a team of potholers to bring out the body. Anyway, after the accident lots of the local kids—including Christian—used to go down to the cave out of morbid curiosity. So the council ended up putting the mesh over the hole and barring the entrance to the cave.

Lately, since his wife's death, Christian had been in the habit of taking long walks by himself, sometimes from early morning until dusk. Then just the other day he'd been on one of his walks when he realized he was on the path that ran near the cave. It was only later, while we were taking the body through the forest, that it occurred to him that maybe they'd filled in the hole or it would be too small to get the body down. "But in the end we were lucky," Christian murmured as he stared into the empty fireplace.

We were silent for a good while but then I asked Christian about his wife. I was curious about her for some reason. Christian told me she'd been a teacher, a primary school teacher, but she'd given that up two years ago when she'd discovered they couldn't have children—she'd found it too painful being around kids every day. She'd been unemployed for a while then eventually went back to university, to do an M.A. Is that where she met her lover, I asked. Yes, he replied tonelessly, the guy's a lecturer. He was at the funeral too. Christian twisted up a beer mat and tossed it at the fireplace. "It's all finished now. I've written to Jamie, I've resigned. I want to travel for a while. West Africa maybe. Anywhere except England."

We stared at each other without embarrassment for another long moment. But then Christian started rambling on, in short phrases, almost like someone talking in his sleep. "Intolerable at first . . . in the morning wishing for the evening . . . in the evening wishing for the morning . . . it all grinds on and on . . . dreams of her not being able to breathe properly . . . but it's strange. In a way I'm not sad about it anymore. I don't know why."

We walked back to the car, barely aware of each other. A dull silence reigned on the journey back to London, the monotonous hum of the engine mesmerizing me, sucking in my thoughts until there was nothing left but a kind of abstract contemplation. At one point I saw Christian blink then try and rub the exhaustion out of his eyes. We climbed a slight incline and accelerated into the valley stretched out before us. It was getting dark though and all you could see was a lonely snake of car lights, trailing into the blackness toward the city.

Then all of a sudden, just after the Slough turnoff, Christian said, "I'd always thought you were a cold bastard. Never said much. I used to wonder how you ended up working in human rights. I didn't really like you."

I tried to remember my initial impressions, if any, of Christian. I recalled that when we'd first met he'd been wearing that same suede jacket he'd had on the day of his wife's death. I said, "I didn't think much about you. I didn't like you or dislike you. Maybe you rubbed me up the wrong way. I probably thought you were a loser."

"I know. I knew that's what you thought."

There was silence again. I remembered something that had happened just before the Jarawa campaign had been launched. I'd been in my office, and a call from some guy in Senegal had been put through to me. But with my pidgin French I couldn't understand a word he was saying. Eventually I'd had to say, "*Je suis désolé mais je ne parle pas français.*" Just at that moment Christian had walked into the office. He'd looked at me in surprise and asked if I needed any help. Christian speaks fluent French. Everyone assumes I do too, because of Marianne. If Jamie had realized I didn't, he might well have given the Jarawa campaign to Christian, and not me.

I stared out the window. A car had drawn up beside us in the other lane. It was a Mercedes and there was only the driver in it. He had one hand on the steering wheel and with the other he seemed to be conducting an imaginary orchestra. It looked kind of dangerous. Suddenly the Mercedes pulled out in front of us and then it was gone.

An instant later we were back in London, turning into Hol-

land Road. That was where my car was. It must have been getting on now, eight-thirty maybe. Christian found a parking space
right outside the block of flats where the bedsit was. I got out
and stared up in horror at this building that seemed to be pushing its way out of the ground and surging up into the dark London sky like some kind of nightmare congealed in stone.
Christian walked me up the road to my car. He asked me if I was
all right and I said yeah. He asked me if I thought I could drive
okay and I said yeah. Then he said he'd better get going. There
were still things I wanted to say to him but it was difficult. "It
isn't what you thought. It isn't that."

"Of course not."

He probably didn't realize what I was talking about. He
probably thought I was trying to tell him that I hadn't killed the
guy. But it wasn't that at all. What I'd actually meant was that I
wasn't paying him back for making me identify his wife's body. I
hadn't called him up for that. Perhaps he understood me after all,
I don't know. I felt incredibly lonely all of a sudden. I didn't want
Christian to go. I tried to spin out the good-byes. "What was it
you'd wanted to talk to me about? That time in the pub. What
was it you kept ringing me up about?"

He shrugged his shoulders. "It doesn't matter anymore . . .
not now."

I nodded. "No, it doesn't matter now."

I was trembling with emotion as we shook hands for the first
and maybe the last time. Christian turned 'round and strode off
into the blackness and I got into my car. There was every chance
I'd never see him again. I sat there for some time trying to com-
pose myself and wondering if I really was able to drive. I looked
at my watch. It still said three o'clock. I'd forgotten it had
stopped. The watch was a fake Rolex someone had bought for
me in Thailand. I took it off and tossed it out of the window.

Almost immediately I heard the crunch of a car running over it. I stuck the keys in the ignition and the engine coughed and started.

Now I was back at the house. Marianne was lying on the couch and she turned right 'round, looking up at me quizzically. "Where've you been?"

"Nowhere."

"Is everything all right?"

I didn't answer, I just stood there. She got up and put her arms 'round my shoulders. "I called you at the office but they said you weren't there. . . . God, you stink of cigarettes. Have you started smoking again or something?"

"Yes."

I noticed that she was wearing the skirt that had been on the back of the chair at the bedsit, the one the man had put away in the drawer. I shivered and couldn't speak for a moment.

Marianne was being very solicitous. She heated up some dinner and asked me if I wanted a drink first and I said yeah. It was peculiar that she was acting like this, since things had been so tense between us lately, but I didn't think too much about it. I didn't have any room for it. It even took me awhile to realize that since Marianne was wearing that skirt, it necessarily meant that she'd been back to the bedsit since Christian and I had been there. I wondered when exactly she'd arrived. Perhaps only minutes after we'd left. In any case it had been a near thing, because it would have had to have been before she picked Jessica up from the day care center. Had she noticed the shiny patch on the floor? And what had she made of the missing vase? Or had she failed to notice it? No, that's not possible. She has an artist's eye.

I ate in silence, with Marianne looking at me reflectively from the other side of the table, her elbows resting on the edge and her chin in her hands. At first I hadn't wanted to eat, but after a couple of mouthfuls I felt a raging hunger and started shoveling the food into my mouth. Then after a minute or two I slowed down again to a more civilized pace. My mind had been spinning on as I ate: it had occurred to me that when Marianne eventually found out about the man she might connect it with my odd behavior tonight. So I thought I'd better try to act as normal as possible. I asked Marianne about her day and so on. The sense of shock faded in and out a little, and right now I started feeling a bit more self-composed. In fact, it surprised me how normally I could carry on once I set my mind to it. I listened to Marianne's lies but they didn't cause that horrible ache they normally did. Maybe because I was lying too. Maybe because I could see now how easy and above all how natural it was for people to lie. I could forgive her that much at least.

We went and sat on the sofa and Marianne got me another drink. Then she put her head in my lap for a while and I stroked her head, combing my fingers through her hair. Eventually she sat up and started kissing me, but I pulled away a little. I didn't want to hurt her feelings though so I said: I appreciate you being this way with me but I still feel funny about things, after what you said the other night. Marianne nodded. She said I understand that—but we're both going to make an effort now, aren't we? We'll try to understand each other's needs. Yes, I replied, we'll both make an effort.

I went into the bedroom and got undressed then went through to the bathroom. I put the shower on as hot as I could take it and stood under the jet of water. It pummeled my back and felt good. I noticed for the first time that I was aching all over and that I had a deepish cut on my forearm. I couldn't think how I'd got it. Perhaps it was the glass from the vase. I washed it clean.

I wished I could stop the exhausting flow of thoughts but I knew that it wasn't possible. The steam was gradually filling the shower cubicle until I could barely see my hands in front of me. I wanted to save Marianne from the horror of it and that meant she must never discover the truth. Of course, that would require a specific sacrifice on my part, which was this: If the man simply vanishes into thin air then in a way he'll never die for her. He'll remain a mystery that will only grow with time. The man will always be there between us, in a kind of stasis. But perhaps that's my punishment.

I was in the shower a long, long time, first just standing there, then scrubbing and scrubbing like mad, then just standing there again. I hadn't even had the grace to thank Christian, it upset me terribly that I hadn't even apologized for getting him involved. It had me almost in tears and I tried to blank it out of my mind. Marianne would find out in the end of course, how could I think otherwise. In any case, she'd discover something. She'd have to tell the police about the bedsit eventually, and then they'd find forensic evidence of one sort or another. Perhaps Marianne would even become a suspect. Perhaps I'd have to turn myself in, precisely to save her.

Eventually I turned off the shower taps. I felt warm and clean but unclean at the same time. I could hear Marianne listening to music in the sitting room, which she often does at night. There was this terrible weariness in me, a total bodily exhaustion I'd never felt before. It was so good to finally escape the relentless-ness of my thoughts and retreat into bed—I was momentarily invaded by this feeling of security that I'd dredged up from my childhood. Beside the bed was something Marianne was read-ing, a battered copy of Pascal's *Pensées*. As a student I'd written an essay about it but that seemed very far away indeed. I flicked through the pages, too tired to decipher much of the French. I tried to remember what it was that might have interested me about this book but it was hard. It was like trying to resurrect a person I'd killed off years ago.

Then another wave of tiredness submerged me. It felt as if all the events of the day were crushing me into unconsciousness and it was impossible to resist. The book slipped from my fingers and I knew that I would sleep a dreamless sleep. It was as if I were falling toward some kind of death.

X

JO CALLED OUT TO ME AS I PASSED BY HER OFFICE. "HEARD THE
news? Jarawa lost his appeal. They've fixed the execution date.
Twenty-second of August."

"The twenty-second? But that's my birthday. It can't be
true."

Her words had a weird physical effect on me, winding me
like a sudden blow to the stomach. I must have gone pale as well
because Jo was looking at me strangely. "Are you okay?"

"Yeah, I'm fine. Just a little dizzy. I need some water or something."

"Come in. Sit down for a minute."

Jo poured me water from a plastic bottle. I drank it slowly
and we didn't say anything for a while. I glanced over the tiny
office space she'd been allocated. She'd made an effort with it

though; she'd made it feel homely. There was a Japanese print on the wall, potted plants, a framed photo of her parents on the desk. I hadn't bothered to do anything like that with my much larger office. I hadn't appropriated it in the same way. I couldn't help feeling that this fact diminished me in some way but in any case it was too late now. It was too late for the photo of Marianne and Jessica on the desk. For a second or two a feeling of intense loss swept over me but then it was gone before I had time to wonder where it had come from and what it meant.

I could feel Jo's curiosity burning into me as I drank the water. Finally she asked if I was all right again and I said yeah. I could tell she wasn't satisfied with that, but she didn't say anything more about it for the moment. Instead she handed me a page she'd printed off from some news website, with the announcement about Jarawa's execution. It also mentioned that he'd been moved from police detention to a notorious prison outside the capital, used solely for lifers and condemned men, nicknamed "Paradise" because no one is supposed to return from it. Once again there was that old photo of Jarawa, like some icon I was seeing everywhere.

Jo and I talked for a while about strategy. It was the first time we'd discussed anything in detail for ages. In fact we'd barely talked at all since I found out about Marianne. I let Jo run on to begin with, since in a way I was still trying to digest the news about Jarawa. I found it almost impossible to believe that they'd actually announced the execution date. I'd always assumed that if they did kill him, news of the execution would surface only once it had taken place. Why had I assumed that? Perhaps because shameful acts are generally committed in secret. Instead they were announcing it as if it were an upcoming spectacle. Maybe that's exactly what it was.

Jo was wondering out loud whether she should cancel the trip to Paris that she'd lined up for the summit of French-speaking countries. She kept rubbing her face and fingering a scar she had high up on her forehead by the hairline. When she rubbed it, it went from white to red. I was listening to her and making suggestions, but at the same time I was remembering an incident from a year, maybe fourteen months ago. It was just after Jo had been taken on. Previously she'd been doing some work for some other human rights organization on the Samson Peters case. Peters had been found guilty of a double murder in the state of Texas and had been sentenced to death. The date for his execution had been set on several occasions but each time his legal team had got a postponement. Once, Peters had been only minutes from death when the stay of execution had finally come through. Eventually DNA evidence proving his innocence came to light and he was pardoned. There'd been a TV program about the case in which Peters had talked about how he'd felt during those hours before the stay of execution, how he'd refused to give up hope, how he'd fought for his life every inch of the way. And yet not too long after being released, Peters had killed himself—his wife had found him hanged in the bathroom, his face turned to the door.

I remembered coming into the office one day to find that Jo hadn't done something important I'd asked her to do. When I'd asked her why she'd suddenly burst into tears. Later I found out that she'd been extremely upset about Peters' suicide. What I'd found jarring at the time was this emotional reaction to the death of someone she'd never even met. But looking back now that's not how it strikes me at all. Rather it's Peters' suicide itself that seems so odd. Because how could you go and kill yourself after you'd fought so hard to live? How could you do that? It made no sense at all.

I was thinking about that and then we started working out the details for the press conference. Eventually I said if we're going to have the press release ready by lunch, then one of us had better get writing. As I got up to leave, Jo said: By the way, I saw Christian yesterday. He said you'd been in touch. He said you'd spent the day together recently.

"He said that? He said that? What else did he say?"

The words spilled out too fast and Jo looked up at me questioningly. "Not much. He's sold his house. He's staying with friends in Hackney or something. Said he wants to get away for a while. Maybe do some volunteer work in West Africa. He asked me to mention it to people in the office, in case anyone has any ideas. That's why I brought it up."

"No, what I meant is, what else did he say about me?"

"Nothing . . . nothing." She was looking at me strangely again. "Listen, I know it's none of my business or anything, but I mean if there's anything you want to talk about—"

"Like what?"

I put my hand to my chin, ostensibly to rub it but the psychological impulse was more to do with covering my face.

"Well, for a few weeks you hardly come in to work at all . . . when you do you're like a ghost. Now all of a sudden you're in here all the time working twelve hours a day or whatever. I just get the feeling that something's not right."

"There's nothing wrong." It sounded flat and I stumbled on. "You know . . . sometimes there are difficulties . . . personal things . . . you know . . ."

Jo shrugged her shoulders. "Okay. It's your business."

I went back to my office. I considered phoning Christian and almost did but then thought better of it. There'd been several times over the past few days when I'd had to fight an almost irresistible urge to phone Christian. The way I got over it was to close my eyes and sort of stop thinking for a while. It's this strange state I seem to be able to put myself in now. The trouble is I can't control it so well. I've no idea of whether it's going to last a minute or half an hour. But when I snap out of it I feel quite calm. It's as if I'd had eight hours' sleep.

Papers were lying scattered all over my desk. I'd been working on half a dozen things at once—it wasn't so much that I wanted to occupy my mind as to confuse it. Aspects of the Jarawa case surrounded me, submerged me. I noticed the piece of paper where I'd scribbled down the London phone number for Jarawa's wife. I'd already left her several messages and had also sent a letter to the address I'd been given but had had no reply. As I punched in the number on the phone I mentally prepared another message to leave on her machine and it took me by surprise when a female voice answered. I introduced myself but then she abruptly interrupted me. "Look. I did get your messages. I did get your letter and I'm sorry I never got in touch. That was wrong of me. But I'm sure you can understand that I've been very busy. And I decided from the outset not to get involved in any public campaign. All I can say is, I don't think it would be appropriate."

"You don't want to get involved, even if it might help your husband?"

"I don't want to get involved in your campaign, no. Please understand."

There was an unpleasant pause—icy distaste crackled along the line.

"I'm sorry. But I'm not sure that I do understand. I appreciate how terrible things must be for you. . . . The fact is that if you'd only let me, I could explain ways in which you could help your—"

"No. I didn't say I was unwilling to help my husband. I said I didn't want to get involved in any kind of public campaign. Beyond that I don't really feel at liberty to speak. I'm afraid that's all I have to say. Thank you for calling."

She'd hung up on me. Well, of all the . . . I put down the phone and sat back down in my chair—I hadn't even realized that I'd got up from it. I could feel this uncontrollable anger rise up in me and a desire to pick up the phone again and hurl it across the room. Moments later the desire and the anger were quite gone and I felt totally calm. It was these instant mood changes that were so hard to get used to. What did it matter to me if Jarawa's wife didn't want to get involved? What did it matter to Jarawa? Surely he was far from all that now, and somewhere deep within himself. Surely there was nothing further I or anyone else could do for him. But I couldn't stop myself envisaging the horror of his end, and I could see him being led to the execution site, hood on head, almost as if it were me and not him.

I remembered that I still didn't know exactly how Jarawa was to be killed. I remembered also how when I was thirteen or fourteen I'd once seen actual footage of an execution on TV, which I now realized colored all my images of such things. It was a Vietnamese guy kneeling down in the street, hands tied behind his back, and an officer shooting him with a pistol held to his head. It was not so much the brutality of it that had struck me at the time but the matter-of-factness and flatness of it, which was how you knew it was real and not a movie.

After the phone call I had a coffee then went to see Jamie. I had to talk to him about visa applications. Jamie was leaning back on his chair so that it stood balanced only on its two back legs, which was kind of dangerous considering his weight. He was reading some report and chuckling to himself. He glanced up at me briefly and said listen to this will you? He started reading out bits of the report to me. It was about British arms exports to Africa. Apparently there's a new trend in the arms industry: "green" weaponry. Lead-free ammunition, missile propulsion systems that don't use CFC gases, etc. "It's fantastic,"

Jamie was saying. "I mean, where the hell do they go from there? Equal opportunity bombs?"

We talked for a while about sending a representative out to Africa incognito, since all our visa applications had been rejected. Jamie was against it though. He said it was too late in the day for it to do any good now, and we were too tight for money anyway. I felt strangely relieved to hear him say that. The idea that anyone else from Africa Action might get to see Jarawa rather than me perturbed me for some reason. Finally I got up to leave. "I have to get going. I've got the World Service thing."

"Excellent. Now listen . . ." Jamie was rubbing his chin, as if deep in thought. "When are we going to play squash again? We haven't had a game in ages."

"Whenever you want, Jamie."

Then, as I opened the door, he looked up at me as if he'd just had some great revelation, something really incisive to impart to me. But in the end all he said was, "Good to see you back on the ball. Sorted your problems out then?"

"Problems?"

"Your, um, 'domestic' problems."

I nodded slowly. "Yeah. I've sorted them out."

I drove to Bush House, taking a detour to avoid Marble Arch for some reason. As I drove an almost intolerable gnawing tension was building up in me—I could feel an oily sweat on my palms as I gripped the wheel and I wiped my hands on my trousers at the red lights.

I couldn't stop thinking about Jarawa's lost appeal and the execution now set to take place on my birthday. These two things seemed to bear down on me with all the weight of a personal failure. An image of Jarawa lying on a trolley in a morgue floated into my mind. The trouble was that I couldn't keep him dead for long. He kept opening his eyes and smiling; he wanted to talk. I even opened my mouth to say something to him, but then I remembered where I was and what I was doing. I pulled over for a minute or two and kind of slapped myself about the face, as if to wake myself up. It was true, I was very tired, I hadn't been sleeping properly. In my mind's eye I could still see the morgue trolley, which I realized was the same as the one Susan Tedeschi's body had been on. It was fitted with a little headrest, as if to keep the body as comfortable as possible. It occurred to me that it must be somebody's job to design those trolleys, with their little headrests.

I'd arrived at the studios. A nervous young Oxbridge type, a trainee maybe, came down to reception to get me. "Gosh, you're cutting it a bit fine aren't you?"

"Really? What's the time?"

"Twenty-five past six."

"Sorry. I got held up. Could you just show me where the loos are before we go up?"

"Umm, you'd better make it quick. You're on in five minutes."

I splashed some water over my face and head and stared into the mirror, cursing myself for leaving no time to prepare. It's been like this ever since my watch stopped working. I even contemplated pulling out of the program, but then it was like I could see Jarawa's face instead of my own in the mirror. The paradoxical idea struck me that although it was my job to campaign for his reprieve, perhaps I'd in fact got things the wrong way 'round. Perhaps it was Jarawa who was watching over me. To what end? All of a sudden I felt better though, and I shook my head like a dog, to get the water out of my hair.

The Oxbridge type hustled me into the studio. The presenter was there—he was already talking—and on the other side of the room sat a big black guy with a shaved head. I recognized him at once, of course. He was the official I'd talked to at the embassy, the day I'd found out about Marianne.

The presenter was talking about Jarawa, then he introduced us and asked the embassy official a question. The guy started speaking in this very smooth, hypnotic tone. He was plying the same line as before—how Jarawa had been found guilty of a criminal and not a political offense. Then he started on about the arrogance of Western governments and organizations. He turned to me. He seemed to be accusing me in an almost personal way: It's your arrogance, he was saying, thinking you have the right to interfere, an arrogance that is simply exacerbating the situation, making it even more likely that miscarriages of justice will occur. . . .

I let him go on for a while in this vein before interrupting him. A flow of words seemed to emanate from me without my quite knowing where it came from. I heard myself saying: He's carrying on as if *I* were the one who was condemning people to death, as if *I* were the murderer. . . . The man tried to speak again, but I could feel the adrenaline prickling under my skin and I raised my voice. My own fluidity astonished me, but even as I marveled at it the words started to dry up and I began to stutter. Now the man was smiling, no longer trying to cut in. I could feel the presenter watching me as well. A reflection of myself stared back from the glass wall that divided the studio from the mixing desks. It was a disturbingly alien face, with holes instead of eyes.

I found myself talking again. The human rights issues are much broader, I was saying. For instance, we know for a fact that Mr. Jarawa has been tortured. . . . I went into some detail about the kinds of torture he might have been subjected to. I was just rehashing descriptions from reports I'd read while covering the Truth and Reconciliation hearings in South Africa. But the fact was that I had no idea whether or not Jarawa had been tortured. Jo and I had certainly discussed its likelihood and had tried to get information from our contacts on the ground, but that was as far as it had gone. I was speaking with a real passion though, I was hot with affront and for a minute or two I really was sure that Jarawa had been tortured. I turned to the man, expecting a denial. He was simply smiling at me though, and it felt like there was everything in that smile.

There was Frank and Phil's housewarming so I went straight home from the studios. But the house was so dark and deathly quiet that at first I wondered whether Marianne had gone. Left for good I mean, taking Jessica with her. The thought didn't make me feel anything in particular. It was this numbness that had cut me off from home life for days now. I opened the door to Jessica's room. She was still there. Her little bedside lamp was on, which is how she likes to sleep. I stood there for a long time watching her as she breathed and snuffled and murmured occasionally. She was in her banana-pattern pajamas, lying on the bed instead of tucked up in it which was unusual. The bedroom was a mess as well, with clothes and toys and picture books lying haphazardly all over the place. It was odd because Marianne usually puts everything away and makes sure the room is tidy before putting Jessica to bed. I noticed the teddy bear abandoned in a corner. His head was hanging on by only a thread now and the stitching of his mouth had come unpicked as well, giving him a lopsided sneer.

The lights were off in the rest of the house and the door to our bedroom was closed. I opened it, half-expecting to find nobody there. Marianne was in bed. She was wearing some old night-gown when she normally sleeps naked. She wasn't asleep though; she was just staring up at the ceiling. Her face looked puffy and tear-stained, but I couldn't really be sure in the half-light.

"What's the matter? Not feeling well?"

"No."

"You're not coming to Frank and Phil's then?"

"No."

"Anything I can get you?"

"No."

I shut the door, walked through to the kitchen. There was a mess of dirty plates and saucepans in the sink. A couple of empty wine bottles stood on the sideboard. Marianne must have drunk both. I got another bottle off the rack and hunted about for the corkscrew. But I couldn't find it, and after I'd looked in all the obvious places I started going through the kitchen drawers. Then I opened this cupboard that's like a junkyard of broken stuff and things we hardly ever use. I had half an idea that we had a spare corkscrew in there. I stuck my hand right down to the back and I could feel something small and cold and curved. I recognized the feel of it; I recognized the way it fitted into my hand. It was a Zippo lighter. I pulled it out and then I stood up and got out the other one from my pocket—the one I'd taken from the bed-sit—and compared the two. They were pretty similar, it was true, but nonetheless recognizably different. And the one I'd just dug out from the back of the cupboard was definitely the one Marianne had given me.

I poured myself a whisky and drank it down then poured myself another. I stared at Jessica's drawing of the man with huge eyes, now pinned to the wall above the kitchen sink. Then I opened the back door and sat down on the back step and got out my cigarettes. I'm still smoking the French brand the man smoked, I don't know why. When I went to the newsagent's afterward, those were the ones I automatically asked for and now I'm used to them.

There was the slightest of chills in the air and a gray mass of clouds slid slowly across the sky. There'd been the flashbacks of course, but apart from that I'd hardly thought about the dead man until now. I'd been living in some kind of animal present, focused on Jarawa and the campaign. I'd hardly even thought about Marianne. And yet all that time I knew of course that *he* was there. He was waiting outside but looking in, threatening to enter at any moment. Perhaps only now was I coming out of the shock. For the moment I was thinking about the mix-up with the lighters. It was clear in my head that if I hadn't made that mistake—if I hadn't been so damned sure that the man's Zippo was the same one Marianne had given me—then I never would have killed him. How strange to think that a man's life could hinge on such a trivial mistake. I just sat there smoking my cigarette staring into the night sky. If I'd only had the nerve to have it out with Marianne, the man would still be alive today. But I'd had weeks to do that and I hadn't. Suddenly I started torturing myself with all these hypotheticals. If only I'd done this, then that would have happened, and if only that had happened, it would never have come to this, and so forth. It lasted for a while, for two cigarettes maybe. But then in the end I got tired of it.

I found myself slipping back into this horrible self-pity that I knew was all wrong, about the Zippo and chance, how I'd been a victim of fate. But I realized soon enough that I was still kidding myself. I started thinking about how I'd put myself beyond the pale and how I wasn't normal anymore, how I was a murderer and everything, how perhaps I'd been a murderer all my life, how maybe this was always going to happen from the very moment I was born or even conceived.

It was the loneliness as well. For the first time since I'd found out about the man, I could feel a wrenching need for physical closeness. I wanted to hold Marianne and comfort her and have her comfort me. I wanted to lose myself in our intimacy. I wanted to touch her body and stroke her hair, although I didn't want to make love. I just wanted to lie with her. I remembered the way she'd walk around the house naked and drunk, at ease with herself and my desire for her.

Something rustling in the bushes interrupted my thoughts. I looked up and for a split second I engaged with the reflective, alien eyes of some small animal, probably a cat, before it disappeared into the night and broke the connection for ever.

Eventually I got up and went to bed. Marianne was no longer staring at the ceiling, she'd turned away on her side. She was asleep, or probably pretending to sleep. I got undressed and slipped in beside her. Her nightdress gave off a musty smell. I lay there rigid, making sure that no part of my body touched any part of hers. It wasn't that my yearning for physical intimacy had in any way diminished, but the closer I actually got to Marianne, the more impossible it seemed. I was thinking about whether she'd found out, and what exactly she'd found out. Things I hadn't even allowed myself to think before. I felt a terrible weight of guilt, although less on account of what I'd done to the man than what I'd done to Marianne. All my efforts to ensure that it wasn't her who found the body counted for nothing—in fact, they were almost acts of vanity.

It surprised me to realize that I'd never felt guilty about anything in my life before. Of course, I'd felt it in theory. I'd felt sorry, and there were plenty of times in the past when I could see that I'd been in the wrong and that I had to make amends. And yet this was entirely different. This was like being possessed by something. It was as acute as sexual desire. I stared at Marianne's back. I knew she wasn't really asleep, because when she sleeps she has this very gentle snore—an adult version of Jessica's snuffling. I longed to turn to her and comfort her. The intolerable thing was that it was me who was the cause of her suffering. It was me who was inflicting the pain. I could hardly be both torturer and consoler. Such a combination was quite grotesque.

Eventually I began to drift off to sleep, but for the first time since I was a child I found myself afraid of what it might bring. The image of Jessica's teddy bear came back to me with its partly detached head. I thought about how tomorrow I could sew him up for her, and how she would appreciate that. It made me feel strangely better, thinking about that.

XI

A BLAZING LIGHT FLOODED THE ROOM THOUGH WE NORMALLY slept with the curtains closed. I could feel this sense of terrible foreboding as I struggled out of sleep, as though something unutterable and infinitely humiliating was about to happen to me—I didn't know what it was but I had no power to stop it. Then as the sleep cleared from my mind I gradually realized that I did know what it was, because it had already happened. It was too late.

Marianne was sleeping profoundly now. Her mouth was open and she was dribbling a little; one of her arms flopped gracelessly over the edge of the bed. She seemed so lifeless that I wondered if she'd taken sleeping pills, as she used to when I first met her. I glanced at my wrist, but I'd forgotten that I no longer had a watch and I swung up out of bed.

Standing under the shower I found myself thinking not about the man or Marianne, but about Jarawa. A problem had arisen at work, an awkward matter, which was the reason I'd phoned his wife yesterday. I'd opened the mail the other day and in an envelope with a South African stamp I'd found a photocopy of a clipping from what seemed like some local African newspaper, dated June 1997. That would have been when Jarawa was already at the UN. The article reported that Jarawa had separated from his wife. It also mentioned rumors that she had shown up one night at a hospital at two in the morning with a cracked rib and covered in bruises. I hadn't yet shown the article to anyone and the question now was what to do with it. A lot of the African press is notoriously partisan and libelous but to research the story and rebut it would obviously mean bringing it to light in the first place, which could do harm. And then there was the probability that the sender had posted it to other organizations.

I was thinking about that and all the things I had to do at work when I realized it was Saturday. I didn't have to go to work. In fact, I couldn't go to work. Marianne mostly looks after Jessica during the week and then on Saturday it's supposed to be my turn. It struck me now that all those Saturdays when I was looking after Jessica and taking her to the park and taking her shopping and buying her ice creams, Marianne had probably been with the man, in the bedsit. The difference was that I didn't want to hurt her anymore because of it. It wasn't because the man was dead or even that I was the one who'd killed him. It was something else.

I got dressed and went through to Jessica's bedroom. She was already up, sitting on the floor, talking to her doll and walking her up and down. "She's getting married. Look, she's getting married today."

"Who's she getting married to?"

"I don't know."

It was still early. I made Jessica's bed then tidied up a bit and started to dress her while she resisted passively. After that we went into the kitchen and I got her some breakfast, which she ate, after a fashion, while I cleared up then did the washing up, slowly so as not to break anything. Everything seemed to require so much thought and attention now, even the daily chores.

"So what do you want to do today? Go up to Battersea Park and see the wallabies?"

Jessica was being unusually quiet. "Where's Maman?"

"Mummy's not well."

"I want to be with Maman today."

"Well you know you can't. On Saturdays we leave Mummy on her own because she needs time to herself."

"I want to be with Maman."

I crouched down to her level. It was this feeling of power-lessness faced with her and it hurt me that she wanted to be with Marianne when normally she looked forward to our Saturday excursions.

"How about I fix Teddy for you? Sew his head back on."

"Where's Maman? Is Maman dead?"

"Of course she's not dead. Whatever gave you that idea? She's in bed."

"I want to be with Maman. I don't want to be with you."

"Why not?"

She suddenly jumped down off her chair and started running toward the door. I grabbed her hand and jerked her back quite brutally, it must have hurt her. I hadn't meant to do that and she screamed. I looked up to see Marianne standing in the kitchen doorway. Weirdly it took me a moment to register and recognize her. Her grayish nightgown hung listlessly off her shoulders and her face was lined and ghostly.

"What are you doing to her?"

"She wanted to wake you up. I was trying to stop her."

I let Jessica go now: she ran over to Marianne, put one arm around her mother's knees, and sucked the thumb of the other hand.

"Well I'm awake now." Marianne's voice was flat. She hoisted Jessica into her arms and whispered something French into her ear. She said coolly, "I'll look after her today. You go and do whatever it is you have to do."

I wondered what exactly she meant by that, but I didn't say anything. I didn't want to talk. I wasn't in the mood for any kind of confrontation. I just picked up the car keys and went out the door.

There were some letters in the letterbox although it was too early for the postman to have come by: they must have been from the day before. It was another symptom. Picking up the mail is one of those things Marianne never forgets to do: her checks arrive by mail and she still writes to people in France. I glanced through the bills and letters and immediately recognized Christian's spidery, boyish scrawl on one of the envelopes. I put the rest of the letters back in the letterbox and tore the envelope open. There was a check inside. I pulled the envelope apart, but there was nothing else in it, not a note or even a return address marked on the outside. The check was made out for sixty pounds. For a moment it mystified me, but then I remembered the night I'd met Christian in that pub in Camden and how I'd paid for his hotel and given him money to get home. Now he'd sent a check to cover my expenses. I ripped it up, got in the car and stuffed the bits in the car ashtray.

At first I thought I'd go into work, but then once I'd started the car all I ended up doing was driving around South London, thinking, smoking. I was thinking about the dead man. I spent a long time reflecting on why he'd died so quickly, when all I'd done was hit him with a not very heavy glass vase. I couldn't see how that could have been enough to kill him within minutes. For a while I played with the idea that a piece of glass must have lodged itself somewhere vulnerable, in his jugular vein for example, but then finally I came up with a more likely explanation. The floor was tiled, he must have slipped and his head had come down hard on the tiles, fracturing his skull, causing fatal internal bleeding. For a moment or two this reading of the events seemed like a revelation and I congratulated myself for my acuity. It suited me to think that it was not the vase but slipping on the tiles that had killed him. It took away some of my own blame, if only an extremely minute part of it.

The sound of a siren cut through my thoughts. I glanced at the rearview mirror: a police car was signaling for someone to pull over and it was a second or two before I realized that it was me. Then it struck me that some time before—maybe a half an hour ago but I couldn't be sure—I'd been vaguely aware of a police car behind me for a good few minutes, almost as if it had been following me. . . . I pulled over abruptly. One of the policemen had got out of the car and was walking toward me, but he seemed to be moving in slow motion and it felt like I had minutes, even hours to consider my response. Of course there would be no question of doing anything stupid. And there would be no question of lying. I swallowed, but my throat was dry and it was painful, then I wound down my window.

"Could I see your license please?"

I made a show of rummaging around my glove compartment. "I'm afraid I don't have it on me. I must have left it in my wallet at home."

"You know that driving without your license in the car is an offense?"

"I didn't know that. I thought I had twenty-four hours to produce it."

The policeman was silent for a moment. He looked away, seemed to stare into space, then turned back to me. "You just went straight through a red light. Do you realize that?"

"No. I didn't realize that."

"Wait there, please." He went back to the police car. I could see him conferring with his partner, who then started speaking into a walkie-talkie. This all took around five minutes or so, then eventually the first policeman came back. "Okay. So I'm going to have to ask you to get out of your car and accompany us to the station."

"You want me to just leave my car here?"

"You can either leave it here or my colleague can drive it back to the station for you."

We walked over to the police car. The policeman had me put my hands against the car and watched as his partner searched me peremptorily. After that I made to get in the back of the car but the policeman said, "Can you get in the front please?"

I watched him as he drove. He was about my age and had fine blond hair and two small pimples in the left-hand corner of his mouth. He didn't seem nervous, but it was hard to tell. At one point the car radio broke into a crackle of interference and incoherent South London dialect, to which the policeman replied laconically, "Okay . . . it's an SR104, St. John's Hill, the usual."

We passed by the low wall of a cemetery. Its stunted forest of gray headstones sprouted up out of the hard ground, stone saplings that had struggled and died. I tried to concentrate and prepare myself for what was going to happen next, but nothing came to mind. I could feel a dull throb in my finger and I held it up to the light to examine it: there was a hairline cut on the tip

and a little dried blood, which I rubbed off. It was a paper cut—
I must have got it opening the envelope from Christian. I started
thinking about him and the check he'd sent me. If he'd done it
before the bedsit there would have been nothing odd about it,
but sending the check afterward hit me hard. It was like a final
settling of accounts, a definitive sign that he wanted nothing further to do with me. It was ridiculous to think of it now, but I
couldn't stop myself.

I wondered how I could explain everything to the police
without mentioning Christian and realized how impossible that
would be. For a start, I would never be able to find the cave in
the forest on my own. It was only now that the reality of this
problem really hit home. I couldn't keep Christian out of it, anymore than I could keep Marianne out of it. Then there was Jessica. Among other things, she'd grow up fatherless. But perhaps
she'd already sensed this truth. Perhaps in her way she'd been
more prescient than any of us—me, Marianne, or her lover. Perhaps she was already preparing herself for this new life, through
her newfound antagonism toward me.

"So what's the procedure? Why do I have to go to the station?"

We were stopped in traffic, but the policeman didn't take his
eyes off the road. "Going through a red light is a serious offense."

"And you do this every time someone breaches the traffic
code? You pull them in?" He didn't answer. After a minute of
silence I continued. "I mean, if you pulled in everyone you
caught speeding or going through red lights, the system would
pretty soon collapse under its own weight, wouldn't it? I mean,
what about the real crimes? What about all the unsolved mur-
ders out there?"

"Hey. I'm trying to drive."

I'd been about to come out with even more ridiculous

things, but I'd caught myself in time. I fell into a kind of reverie. Then after an eternity, the policeman said, "We've got to breathalyze you."

"You're taking me in just to breathalyze me?"

"Yeah."

The car radio had broken out into a confusion of voices again, but this time the policeman didn't answer. We'd arrived at the police station, a squat gray box of a building that resembled a miniature prison. Inside there was a large room with a row of counters behind a glass front, like in a bank or a dole office. We stopped there a moment while the policeman picked up a form from one of the counters, then he led me through a side door, down a corridor, and into another much smaller room. It had a big metal door and you could tell that it had been a cell once. The policeman told me to wait there until my name was called, then walked off. I sat down on one of the plastic chairs. It was the same garish shade of orange as the ones at the hospital waiting room where I'd identified Susan Tedeschi's body.

There were two other people in the room. a woman of around twenty-five and her blond-haired son, who was about the same age as Jessica. He had a strangely elfin-looking face that both charmed and disturbed. He was watching me with naked, childish curiosity. I smiled at him, but he looked away nervously. I reached into my jacket pocket and pulled out a pencil. On the top it had an eraser in the shape of a grinning little banana man. Jessica was collecting them. There were all kinds of fruit people and you got them from petrol stations. I pulled the rubber off the pencil, put it on my little finger and jiggled it up and down. The boy looked up in shy fascination. Then I took the banana man off my finger and put it on the boy's. I'd been saving it for Jessica.

The boy said. "What's his name?"

"I don't know."

"What's he do?"

"Nothing."

His mother cut in. "Leave the man alone, love."

She was flicking nervously through a newspaper. I looked over her shoulder and a headline caught my eye. "Mystery Disappearance of Oxford Professor." I looked away immediately, through the window high up in the corner. You could still see the discolored patches on the windowsill, where the bars had once been. The boy was holding the little banana man and tugging at his mother's dress. "Look! Look!" The woman put down her newspaper to remonstrate gently with the boy, who started to suck his fingers defensively. "Take your fingers out of your mouth, love." When he did, you could see corns where the skin was almost broken.

I asked the mother if I could look at her newspaper and she handed it to me wordlessly. I skimmed through the first few pages to make it look like I was just idly reading then eventually I turned to the story that interested me. There were just three short paragraphs. "Renowned historian" Richard Weldon had failed to turn up for a lecture a week ago: colleagues had searched his college rooms and then his North Oxford house before calling the police. A full investigation into his disappearance was currently under way but had produced no firm leads as yet. One theory was suicide: Weldon's wife had died recently after a long battle with multiple sclerosis. But friends insisted that he had been coping well with her death and had shown no signs of suicidal tendencies. Weldon was also said to have been involved in negotiations over the fate of a political prisoner in an unnamed African country. Police had yet to rule out a link.

I skimmed through the story again and stared for a minute or two at the grainy, unrecognizable photo of the man—I could hardly remember what he looked like alive anyway, only dead. Then I started reading another article on the opposite page, about a bizarre incident that had happened the other night. Two strangers had been walking across Albert Bridge from opposite directions. When they crossed paths one had suddenly grabbed the other and hauled him over the railings into the river. Being young and a strong swimmer, the victim had survived. His assailant had gone straight to the police station and confessed his crime. What was odd was that not only was the crime motiveless, but the perpetrator was a well-respected doctor with a happy marriage, two children, no history of mental illness, and no financial problems. He had fully cooperated with the police but could offer no explanation for his act. He had, however, expressed a wish to see the person he'd pushed into the river, and the man in question had agreed to a meeting.

I thought about this article for a while. It disturbed me almost more than the one on the man I'd murdered. I wondered what exactly it was that the doctor wanted to say to the man he'd pushed into the river. With some surprise I realized what it was about the story that disturbed me. I was jealous that this man was being given the opportunity to speak to his victim. I folded the paper neatly and handed it back to the woman.

She looked my way. "Do you have a cigarette?"

"Only French ones."

"That's fine."

I gave her a cigarette and lit it for her. She started sucking on it as if her life depended on it, then coughing and sucking on it again.

She said, "So, what are you here for?"

"Oh you know. The usual. First-degree murder."

The woman giggled, then so did the little boy in imitation. In fact he started laughing so hard, in this peculiar, uncontrollable way, that his mother eventually had to tell him to stop.

I continued. "Just a traffic offense actually. Went through a red light."

"Really? They pull people in for that?"

I didn't reply. Eventually a policeman came in to get the woman. I was on my own for a minute or two, then the same guy came back for me. We went down some stairs and along another corridor, past door after door, most of them half-open. Through one of them I could even hear the woman I'd given the cigarette to a few minutes before. She was saying, "You can check it if you want. But it's not an offense if I wasn't soliciting. Listen, I know the laws on this better than you do. . . . "

We stopped at a door at the end of the corridor. There was a name on it. Friedman. The policeman knocked and then signaled for me to go in. A bored-looking guy sat behind a desk. He looked up from the papers he was reading and started asking me a string of questions. Had I had anything to drink in the last twenty-four hours, had I taken any medication or any illegal substances, etc. He picked up the Breathalyzer lying on the desk and asked me to blow into it, which I did. Then he asked me whether I'd be prepared to give a blood sample, if necessary, and I said I would, if necessary. I was wondering about the name on the door, Friedman. It reminded me of something, but it took me a while to remember what it was. It was the name that had been on the little memorial stone inside the cave, where Christian and I had disposed of the body. It occurred to me that maybe the policeman in front of me was related to the little boy who'd lost his life in the cave but there was no way of finding out, short of actually asking the guy. I almost did at one point but then I stopped myself.

"Hello? Are you with me?"

The police guy was looking at me strangely. I hadn't been listening. I'd been thinking of something else.

"I said, is there anything else you want to say to me?"

"Like what?"

"Like anything else."

He was piercing me with this odd stare that was hard to meet, but equally hard to pull away from. "No. No, there's nothing else." We continued to stare at each other for a few more seconds, but then finally he looked back down at his paperwork. "Well you'll have to come back tomorrow with your driver's license. Then you'll receive notice from the magistrate's court sometime over the next few weeks."

I could feel the sweat under my armpits. The guy was writing something and I just stayed there watching him until finally he looked up again. "Okay. You can go now."

I got up slowly. The guy was watching me almost inquisitively and I noticed that my mouth was open, as if I were on the verge of speaking. It was this torturing desire to confess, which was hardly going to go away, quite the reverse. The only way to rid myself of it would be to yield to it, which in due course I would most certainly do. The realization of this came as an unexpected relief, momentarily liberating me from what felt like an intolerable pressure. It was perhaps like the relief of someone who is finally informed that he has a terminal illness, after he'd long suspected it.

I had to fill in a form then queue up and get it stamped by a policeman behind the counter, who handed me my car keys. I walked out through the glass doors, and as soon as I was outside I started taking great gulps of the polluted London air, as if I'd been submerged for minutes and was on the point of drowning. I looked at my left wrist—I kept forgetting that I didn't have a watch anymore. It was something to do with the fact that I had no idea of when I'd murdered the man. I calculated with my fingers. Was it eight days ago, or nine? Sometimes it felt very close, like something that happened an hour ago, then at other times it seemed very far away indeed, like the distant memory of falling in love for the first time.

I stopped a young guy and asked him the time. He didn't reply though, he just looked up at me expectantly and I realized he was actually a beggar. He had a wispy beard and a suede jacket like Christian's. I reached into my pocket, but I had no change on me. Wait a second, I said, there's a cashpoint on the corner. As he followed me there he started talking in a curiously high-pitched voice, wheezing and taking quick, shallow breaths as he did so. I'd work if I could, he said, but I've got this incurable disease, a congenital thing that leaves me short of breath. There's only seventeen other cases like it in the whole of Britain. He said this last bit with evident pride. I got some money out and gave it to him, three twenty-pound notes.

Whispered voices emanated indistinctly from somewhere in the house but it was hard to tell from where exactly. There was a pervasive smell of cigarettes too, the French ones I'd been smoking lately. Had Marianne helped herself to mine or had she bought her own? Clothes, toys, bottles, glasses and dirty plates lay strewn about the sitting room and I started to pick them up out of habit but then I stopped. It was this weird premonition about things and I went into the bedroom, our bedroom. The place was a tip as well. Both of them were in there, Marianne and Jessica. Marianne was still in her gray nightgown although it was about six in the evening now and Jessica was naked, despite the fact that I'd dressed her that morning. She was perched precariously on the dressing table so that she could see herself in the mirror—she was putting on lipstick and rouge and mascara, smearing it all over her face like a hideous mask. The dressing table, which Marianne normally kept immaculately clean and tidy, was a mess of open tubes and pots, some of them knocked over and spilled. Marianne was lying on the bed. She was playing with a doll, the one Jessica had told me was getting married. She was moving its arms and remonstrating with it.

"What the hell's going on here?"

Neither of them looked up. Marianne's nightgown was speckled with purple; at first I thought it was blood but then I noticed a half-drunk bottle of wine by the bed. She'd got through all the stuff we'd bought for day-to-day consumption and now she'd started on the crate I'd laid down the year Jessica had been born. It was supposed to be for Jessica's twenty-first birthday or something.

I strode across the room and picked up Jessica. "Okay. Let's get you cleaned up."

I carried her into the bathroom and ran the bath. The lipstick had somehow got all over her, not just on her face but on her body too, like some kind of warpaint.

I interrogated her as I washed her. "Have you eaten? Did Mummy get you anything to eat?"

"Yeah. We had chocolate doughnuts! And wine."

"She gave you wine?"

"I wanted milk, but there wasn't none."

"Any. There wasn't any."

I got her clean then took her along to her bedroom to get dressed. I could hear Marianne in the other bedroom, still drunkenly talking to the doll bride. Jessica was playing an obscurely malicious game with me as I put her pajamas on. "Where do you live, Daddy?"

"What do you mean? I live here of course."

"No, but where do you live really?"

"Here. I told you. You know that."

"But where do you live, Daddy? Where?"

And so on. She wasn't tired at all and I could see it would be difficult to get her into bed. Then after awhile she changed tack. She was saying, "Did you go to the petrol station today? Did you? Did you?"

"I did. And I've got you something."

I reached into my pocket for the rubber banana man I'd got

for her, but then I remembered that I'd given it to the little elfin-faced boy instead. "You'll have to earn it though. You'll have to go to bed like a good girl then I'll give it to you in the morning."

"I want it now!"

"Well you can't have it now."

"Give it to me!"

She stared at me with menace in her eyes. What was she threatening me with? In what way could she hurt me? But I realized soon enough how weak I was faced with her.

"Listen, why don't I read to you?"

"No!"

"What about your dolls? Do you want to play with your dolls?"

"No!"

"How about Teddy then? Where's Teddy?"

Suddenly she went strangely calm and silent.

"Well? Why don't you go and get Teddy? Where is he?"

She didn't say anything. She was tentatively shaking her head. In fact her whole body was trembling in an odd way.

"Hey. I asked you a question. I asked you where Teddy was."

Still she didn't answer. She was looking at the floor, then I caught her furtively glancing in the direction of the door, as if to calculate her chances of dashing out of the room without me catching her. I grabbed her by the shoulders. "Jessica! What have you done with Teddy? Answer me!"

She mumbled something but in such a tiny voice I couldn't catch it. "What was that? What did you say? I didn't hear you."

"I said he's gone."

"Gone where?"

Her voice seemed to come from a million miles away. "To heaven."

"Heaven? What do you mean?"

"I told you before. The man got him. Teddy got sick."

"Man? What man? What are you talking about?" I was shaking her and almost shouting. "Where's Teddy? Where is he? Show me. Show me what you've done with him, Jessica!"

"In the garden."

She was whimpering and shivering and I could tell she was too scared to cry properly—frightened as to what I might do to her.

"In the garden where? Show me, Jessica. Show me!"

We went out into the garden. She led me to this narrow strip between the fence and Marianne's shed-cum-studio that didn't get any light and had no grass growing on it. Someone had been digging there though and I noticed a delicately constructed little cross impaling the earth, a tiny thing only a few inches high.

"Let go! You're hurting me!"

I was still gripping Jessica and I noticed that my fingers had left little red marks on her shoulder. As I relaxed my hold she pulled away violently and ran back toward the house. I made no effort to pursue her. I stared down at the little plot then got down on my knees and started digging with my hands. The earth was loose and easy to scrape away. I pulled out a wooden box, like a big cigar box. I opened it. Inside was a little figure enveloped in a white tea towel. I unwrapped the teddy bear and held it in my hands. I had this bizarre feeling that it was in fact alive and that I could even feel it pulsating. The thought horrified me for a moment, until I realized that it wasn't the teddy bear that was pulsating but the veins and capillaries in my own fingers. It was hard to make out whether the teddy bear's mouth was grinning or snarling. I put it back in the box.

I sat out in the garden for a while, on the grass. I felt the sharp edge of the cigarette packet in my pocket and got it out and smoked one, although it was difficult to light with my shaking hands. There were storm clouds in the sky and the atmosphere was hot and almost unbearably heavy. I still had the wooden box in my arms, I was cradling it like a baby.

Huge drops of rain started to fall and I got up and went inside. I didn't want to see Marianne and Jessica till I'd calmed down so I got started on the pile of washing-up in the sink. But then I lost interest halfway through and dried my hands and lit another cigarette—I'd been practically chain-smoking ever since the bedsit and could feel it every morning, the wheezing and the nicotine hangover. I looked up at the childish drawing of a man that was pinned to the kitchen wall and that was really not bad and I wondered if Jessica would end up an artist like her mother. It was almost the first thought I'd had about the future since the day of the murder. I continued to stare at Jessica's drawing until I could feel the man's black eyes drawing me in like I was falling into them, into some fathomless well but I didn't know where it was, whether it was there somewhere in the bedsit or in my hands or deep inside me.

I went into the study and opened up the drawer in the desk with all Marianne's stuff in it. I pulled out a notebook—her diary for this year—and started reading, positioning myself so I could easily throw it back in the drawer and pretend to be doing something else should Marianne come in. At first I read through each entry, but since they were mainly abstract remarks about her work I started scanning through them, on the lookout for names, troubled more by what the writing didn't say than what it did. Eventually I came to the last entry. It was dated the day of the murder. A single sentence, marked with an asterisk. "Discussion with R.—agreed and now to tell M." I flicked through the rest of the blank pages then put the notebook back in the drawer. There was relief at the blank pages. Relief that she'd written nothing since that day, but also dread that she would do so eventually and that I wouldn't have the willpower to stop myself reading it.

Now I walked through to our bedroom, the wooden box still under my arm. I thought I was calm, but then as soon as I saw

Marianne and Jessica I lost it again. Marianne was lying propped up on the bed with Jessica beside her. It took me a moment to realize what the situation was, what Jessica was doing. She had her eyes closed and perhaps she was half-asleep, sucking at her mother's breast as Marianne stroked her head and whispered to her.

"For Christ's sake, Marianne . . . She's three years old!"

Jessica had opened her eyes and was looking up at me in fear, her little face pressed close to her mother's shoulder. I was waving the wooden box at them. "What's this? What the hell's this? What are you trying to do to her? What the hell are you . . ."

I could feel a sudden piercing in my head. I closed my eyes and put my hand to my forehead and moaned. It was like a hallucination or something—an image of flames. It lasted I don't know how long then vanished as quickly as it had come . . . with just the orange of the flames remaining with me a little longer. For a moment I thought I was going to vomit, but then that sensation passed too. I opened my eyes, feeling dazed and exhausted and I stared out the window as the rain cried down the panes.

Marianne had got up, Jessica still in her arms, and was walking out of the bedroom. From her pallor and stumbling I could tell she'd not only been drinking but had taken tranquilizers as well. I sat down on the bed then lay down on it. Even in the midst of all this unreality there was some part of me that never ever lost touch, that was coldly observing, interested in some scientific way perhaps to know what exactly was going on, what the mechanics of this disintegration would be and the logic that would dictate the end.

It was light when I'd entered the bedroom and dark when Marianne came back in. She seemed vaguely surprised to see me still there and stared blankly at me for a moment, but then just crashed out on the bed beside me. I shook her to stop her dozing off. "I want to talk to you."

She opened her eyes. They were completely glazed over.

"Nothing left to talk about."

"Yes there is. There's Jessica."

"What do you mean?"

"The teddy bear. The teddy bear."

She was barely conscious, half talking in her sleep and slurring her words. "She wanted to. Nothing to do with me. I helped her. Made the cross. I'm tired. Need to sleep. I took some pills."

"How many?"

"Enough."

"You shouldn't. Not while you're pregnant."

"Doesn't matter. Getting rid of it. Fucking thing inside me."

"You can't do that."

"Don't tell me that. I'm the Catholic. Not you."

I shook her again, quite hard, but I couldn't wake her. I got her into bed and stared at her face as she breathed in this horribly laborious way, as though she were trying to bring something up from deep inside her. I had this vision of waking up in the morning or perhaps the middle of the night and turning to her and her being cold as marble and I knew that I'd have to stay awake now and watch over her. I lit a cigarette. I just kept staring at her. She was becoming more and more alien to me, almost as if she were someone I barely knew at all.

XII

I WAS WALKING PAST AN ITALIAN RESTAURANT 'ROUND THE CORNER
from work. There was a woman in there seated at a window
table by herself. She was sitting stiffly in her chair facing the
window front, drinking wine, although it was only midday, staring at me or perhaps beyond. I glanced her way and for a
moment I was sure that it was Susan Tedeschi. I stopped and
stared, shocked at my own certainty. A dream returned to me.
I'd had it that morning but perhaps on other occasions as well.
In this dream I'm back in the morgue in the hospital in Oxford.
I come in, Susan Tedeschi's lying on the trolley, there's a tag on
her wrist. She opens her eyes and looks up to me and smiles.
Then she props herself up on one elbow and beckons me with
the other hand. Could it be that she wants to kiss me? I'd
woken up in the night shivering and frightened like a child,

disturbed also by the fact that Marianne was no longer there beside me.

The illusion outside the restaurant only lasted a couple of seconds. Because the odd thing was that the woman in the restaurant didn't actually look anything like Susan Tedeschi, apart from the blond hair. For a start, she was maybe ten years too old. Then I realized that I did know this face after all, if only in a secondhand way. I'd seen photographs of it. I'd even filed one away along with the other Jarawa documents.

I went in. She was talking to the waiter and then shook her head. The shock of thinking she was Susan Tedeschi had receded and now I was imagining a conversation with Jarawa. I was imagining telling him how I'd bumped into his wife one day and I could almost see his astonished smile. It was a new thing, these imaginary conversations. . . . Or maybe it was a very old thing. It was like childish behavior.

She looked surprised and put out and left me standing for a few minutes, but then invited me to sit down. We small-talked for a while. She was saying how strange it was to be back in London and how it had changed since she'd lived here. How less English it was now, how it was like any international city, same shops, same cars, same young men in the streets begging. She carried on in this vein for some time, but eventually I cut in. I said that I knew it was difficult, but really I felt obliged to talk about her husband. I said I'd just like her to hear me out one more time, to explain how she could help her husband by getting involved in our campaign. There was a long silence after I'd said my piece.

"Look, I'm afraid I'm going to be blunt. I'm not going to get involved in your campaign. I'm sorry that I was rude to you on the phone, that was inexcusable of me. I'm not getting involved and you'll just have to accept that I have my reasons."

"Okay. But the least you could do was talk to me. You cut me off. You didn't even want to hear what I had to say. I can give you an example right now of one way your involvement might be appropriate. The other day someone anonymously sent us a newspaper clipping, dated a few years back. It was about how you and your husband had separated. It implied that he'd been very violent toward you. I would have liked to talk to you about it. It's likely that this story will come out anyway and it would be better to have a rebuttal ready for release. That's just one thing—"

"Well I can tell you now that I won't be making any statement about my marriage, whatever the circumstances."

"Even if it might affect your husband's fate?"

"Our marriage has nothing to do with his situation now."

"Come on . . . let's not be naïve. You may not live in London anymore, but you know how the world works. You know where PR fits into the picture."

She studied me in silence for a moment, hands clasped beneath her chin. "You're very persistent, aren't you? You're not going to leave me alone, are you?"

"That depends. It depends on what happens to your husband. I'll do whatever I think is necessary."

"Yes. I can see that. Because you're quite like him in a strange kind of way."

"What do you mean?"

I was surprised by what she said and genuinely interested, but she didn't answer. For a second she even looked like she was about to ask me to leave, but instead she poured herself a glass of wine and offered me some. There was an empty glass on the table and for the first time I noticed that there were two table settings.

"If you're allowing some kind of, well let's say resentment, to get in the way of supporting your husband—"

"I think that's a pretty shocking and insulting insinuation to make."

I shrugged my shoulders. "I apologize."

Then all of a sudden she completely lost her cool. All this stuff started spilling out about how her husband had caused her great pain, how he'd been unfaithful from day one and she wasn't about to turn around and say he was a great husband to anyone now. As she spoke, my gaze shifted from her eyes to her arms, which were somehow too thin. I could make out the shape of the bone underneath the sun-parched skin. I'd switched off and in a way this outpouring had the effect of calming me. What was strange was how any intense concentration on Jarawa always brought me back to Marianne's lover, and vice versa. Perhaps the connection was that they both seemed so real now. On the other hand, what seemed phantasmagorical to me was the hole in the cave and the great round boulder outside that was like a lid or a plug. That was what I found hard to believe in. That was what seemed the product of a strained imagination.

Now I switched my gaze back to the woman's eyes. She was still talking, but she'd regained control of herself. She seemed embarrassed by her outburst. She was saying that I'd misunderstood her, that whatever she felt personally, it was of course the principle at stake and that the death penalty was a horrible barbarity that must be opposed. A kind of weariness came over me as I heard those words. So you too, I said, you think he's guilty as well? You as well?

"I've hardly seen him over the last couple of years. I really have no idea of the situation. . . ."

Then she added that she didn't want me to think she wasn't doing anything, but that she didn't feel "at liberty" to tell me exactly how she was involved. . . .

Something about that phrase jolted me. I interrupted. "I think I know what you're up to. Let me guess. You've got your contacts in the government and the military, but it's not safe for you anymore so you've come to London. And you're negotiating for your husband's release through the embassy here. Right?"

She didn't say anything.

"A big guy with a shaved head. And there're some Oxford academics involved as well. Pierre Douff maybe. And Richard Weldon. Certainly Richard Weldon. Right? And he told you not to get involved with us. And so did the big guy with the shaved head."

Now she nodded.

"But Weldon's mysteriously disappeared. Maybe he was only tangentially involved. Nobody's sure whether his disappearance has got anything to do with the Jarawa case. And it's put a spanner in the works. Right?"

"How do you know about all of this?"

I got up from the table. "It doesn't matter. I can tell you something though. Something you can mention to the others. It might help them. Weldon's disappearance has got nothing to do with your husband. That's one thing I'm sure about."

Four in the morning and I can't sleep. It's been strangely calm over the past few days. As if the whole world was in suspension, waiting for something that refuses to happen. I came home the day I saw Jarawa's wife and there was a removal van parked outside the house. But it wasn't what I'd expected. They were moving a bed into the house, not out of it. Marianne was there, guiding the removal guys through the house, out the back door to the garden then into her studio. One or two other things followed—a fridge, a cooker, a table. Then she disappeared and the first time I saw her again was yesterday evening. I don't know what she's doing in there. Sleeping by day and painting by night I think. I can see the light on in the studio from the kitchen window. Actually it's a strange comfort that she's there, just a few yards away from where I am. Because I can be alone only to a certain extent. If she moved right out it would be infinitely more difficult for me. For her too perhaps.

I was back from another BBC interview; I was feeding Jessica. This was yesterday. Jessica was being hyperactive. She often is now and rarely sleeps before eleven at night. I suppose she sleeps with Marianne during the day. She was acting up and refusing to eat and making fun of me. That was good because it meant she was feeling confident of herself and unafraid of me, which was unusual. Usually she gobbles the food in silence and runs back to the studio. She'd been drawing and painting. She'd brought some drawings in from the studio, perhaps to show me or perhaps not.

"Did you do these today?"

"I'm helping Maman. Now she needs me to draw for her."

"I see . . . And who are the people in the pictures? Do you know?"

They were mainly in black and white, vaguely sinister stick figures. She pointed at me, giggling. "You! They're you!"

"What, all of them?"

"Yes!"

"And this is what Mummy asked you to draw? Pictures of me? Or was it your own idea?"

"Yes . . . no . . . dunno . . . " She was playing distractedly with her food. She'd lost interest in the pictures, in our conversation. I noticed a small red mark on her neck that hadn't been there before. I was just about to examine it when all of a sudden she said, "Look at me. Look at me, Daddy. Guess what I'm pretending."

She'd put down the little plastic fork she uses and rested her head on the table. She was staring across the room in this fixed, disturbed way.

"I've no idea, Jess. I don't know what you're pretending. Maybe you're asleep."

"'Course not! You can't sleep with your eyes open, silly!"

"I don't know then. I give up."

"Guess, Daddy."

"I can't guess. Tell me."

"I'm dead. I'm playing a dead person."

"Okay. Stop it. Eat your food. Stop it now, Jessica."

She started chanting. "I'm dead, I'm dead, I'm dead, I'm dead . . ."

"That's enough! I said that's enough!"

I could feel my anger rising like a wave and I leaned over the table in a trance. Perhaps I was about to grab Jessica or something, but the sound of the doorbell sliced through the air and put an end to the madness. Jessica had stopped chanting and sat up and I stood there frozen to the spot. The doorbell rang again. I couldn't think who it could be.

A couple of policemen stood on the doorstep, one tall John Cleese type with a mustache and a smaller, stocky guy. The tall guy said: I'm sorry to disturb you at this hour, sir, but we're looking for Marianne Soubirous. Does she live here?

"What's it about?"

"Are you perhaps her husband?"

"Yeah . . . not exactly . . . we live together."

"We're investigating a disappearance, a man who disappeared from his home in Oxford two weeks ago and hasn't been seen since. We found your partner's name in his address book. No doubt she's not involved in any way but you can understand that we need to contact everyone anyway. . . ."

He didn't have a London accent—in fact he didn't sound like a policeman at all. He sounded like quite a friendly guy. His slight stoop and rounded shoulders reminded me of Christian. Jessica had disappeared somewhere, maybe to her bedroom. I walked back through to the kitchen and opened the back door.

I wasn't thinking straight. Was it relief that the police weren't here for me or was it anger? I walked across the damp grass to the studio. I could hear music coming from inside, howls and distorted guitars. I opened the door. I thought Marianne might be working since she usually works with music, but she wasn't. She was moving around in this weird way. It was hard to make out what she was up to, dancing maybe, or doing exercises. She'd shaved her head. It made her look completely different. I wondered why she'd done that. She'd had such lovely dark hair.

I glanced around the studio. She'd done it up since I'd last been there. She'd painted it and had hung her canvases 'round the walls, crammed the walls with them so they completely dominated the small space. I stared at them. I had the impression that I'd never understood Marianne's work before or perhaps I'd just never really thought about it. Perhaps I'd thought that these canvases were simply fantastic designs. Now I could see quite clearly that they weren't designs at all. The bright colors were in fact a struggle against a fear I'd been only vaguely aware of before. And yet how was it that I'd never noticed this? How could that be?

She stopped writhing around when she noticed me, although not out of embarrassment—she just looked up at me questioningly. It was hard to take her looking at me like that, she looked so raw with her shaved head. I shouted over the music. There's the police at the door, asking for you. She didn't reply. She was dressed in tracksuit bottoms and a thick, shapeless woolly jumper, despite the fact that it wasn't cold at all. She went over to the stereo and turned it off. Then she pulled off her jumper and slipped out of the tracksuit bottoms, without looking my way, and put on jeans, bra, T-shirt. I noticed black paint on her fingertips, like she'd just been fingerprinted or something. She didn't look nervy or anything, although it wasn't calmness either. She looked blank, like she'd just smoked a joint or taken a tranquilizer.

I followed her back through the garden. I wondered what she was going to say to the police, but in a way I couldn't get too interested. It was the small things that so often caught my attention now rather than the larger picture. For instance as we walked I was thinking about the staring eyes Jessica had had when she'd been pretending to be dead. It wouldn't have occurred to me at that age that a dead body might have its eyes open.

The policemen were still there on the doorstep and Marianne invited them in. She was smiling now, it was amazing how she could suddenly turn into someone quite different at whim, and it was something about her that I resented. The police didn't seem at all fazed at her shaved head, but of course they'd never seen her any different. The tall guy, the one who did all the talking, was saying that if Marianne wanted to discuss this in private then there was no need for me to be present, or that if she wanted they'd be happy to come back tomorrow during the day. The small, stocky one just stood there saying nothing. He actually had a notebook in his hand, like a cartoon caricature. No, no, said Marianne, there's no need for you to come back. There's no need for it to be in private.

She led them into the kitchen/dining room and I cleared the table of Jessica's half-eaten sausages. The tall one launched into his spiel again, about how a man had disappeared and how Marianne's name had been found in his address book, etc. As he spoke I watched Marianne, her mask of a face transforming from polite attentiveness to a sort of empathy, almost as if the policeman himself had suffered some loss that he was now unburdening onto us.

The policeman asked Marianne if she knew this man, Richard Weldon, and at first Marianne shook her head; then she said maybe, the name was familiar after all, but she couldn't immediately say why. I'd left a knife on the table and Marianne had unconsciously picked it up and was fiddling with it, turning it 'round in her hands so that sometimes the blade pointed at me, sometimes at one of the policemen, and sometimes at herself. Did she have any idea why her name might be in the man's address book, asked the policeman. Well, said Marianne, I'm an artist. I meet a lot of people, people in the art world and collectors as well. . . . Was this Richard Weldon perhaps a collector? The policeman said he didn't know, he'd look into it, and he got out a photo. Do you recognize him, he asked. Again Marianne shook her head uncertainly. I couldn't say for sure that I don't know him, she said finally. He looks sort of familiar but beyond that I couldn't say. She handed the photo back to the policeman, who then turned to me. And you, sir, he said, have you ever seen this man before?

The photo was blurred, perhaps it was the same one they'd used in the newspaper—it was surprising in a way that they didn't have a better picture. The blurriness of it distorted the man's features, rendered them vaguely indistinct like the image of a ghost. I shook my head. For a moment I couldn't speak, then I said: Never seen him before, I'm afraid. But as soon as I'd said that, I realized that I'd been too forthright in my denial, that Marianne had played the better game. Because no one can ever be too certain that they haven't seen some guy in a blurred photo.

The policemen got up from their chairs. The stocky one got out a card and handed it to the tall one, who then proffered it to Marianne. This is where you can get in touch with us if you remember anything or come across anything that could be relevant, he said. Marianne put the knife back on the table and took the card. Of course she replied and smiled. I accompanied them to the door, leaving Marianne at the kitchen table. Well, thank you for your time, the smaller guy said. It was the first time he'd spoken and his squeaky voice surprised me. Not at all, I replied, and I continued: So who was this guy Richard Weldon anyway? Too late I realized that I'd used the past tense instead of the present. He's a professor at an Oxford college, said the taller one, looking me directly in the eyes. Really, I replied. I'd maybe wanted to ask other questions, but I shut up now after the past tense slip-up. Well, good luck with your inquiries, was all I could think of saying.

I shut the door and waited in the hall until I could hear their car starting up. I went into the kitchen but Marianne had already returned to the studio. I thought of following her out there but then immediately dismissed the idea. The whole thing was too confused and it was impossible to think straight about it. Marianne had been so cool and unruffled with the police, I wondered how she'd managed it. I wondered too why she hadn't told them that Richard Weldon had been her lover, but in a way it didn't seem to matter. Nonetheless, if she had done, I'd certainly have admitted everything as well, there and then, even in front of Marianne, and despite having to implicate Christian. I wouldn't have been able to stop myself.

I checked Jessica's room but she wasn't there. She must have gone over to the studio as well. I was alone in the house. I went into our bedroom then through to the bathroom. I took my clothes off and stood naked by the full-length mirror Marianne had put up—wherever she lives, she always has to have a full-length mirror. I examined myself from head to toe. I was aware that I'd always taken a little too much pride in my body—my pectorals, flat stomach, and the symmetry of it, a sort of blank perfection like a youth in a fascist poster. Nothing had changed, but I could see now what would happen twenty years down the line, if ever I lived that long—the roundness that would eventually turn into a paunch, the thin bony legs, the sagging chest. I remembered the old man that I'd seen at the swimming pool on the day Susan Tedeschi died, and then once again on the day I'd killed Marianne's lover. I couldn't help hoping that it was the last time I'd have to encounter him.

XIII

THERE WAS THE USUAL PILE OF MAIL ON MY DESK: I FLICKED
through it, tossing the boring-looking letters aside for Jo to deal
with. One envelope—slightly crumpled with a colorful stamp, a
crossed-out address and a number of smudged postmarks—
caught my attention. I ripped it open. In my hand was a sheaf of
poor-quality writing paper, covered with a barely legible scrawl.
My eye skipped along the lines, hardly making any of it out. Perhaps it was just another of those crazies who wrote in all the
time, but the lurching of my heart was telling me otherwise.
Then eventually I went back to the beginning and tried to decipher it, word for word, rewriting it in my own clear hand.

The letter was written in not particularly good English, full
of grammatical errors and franglais. He'd heard me on the World
Service and was writing to correct a few false impressions. First

and foremost, he had never been tortured and he wanted me to publicly correct the statement I'd made about that. Conditions in the prison were not good, he wrote, but in his opinion they didn't specifically contravene any UN conventions. In any case they were no worse for him than for any of the other prisoners there—and in some ways were a lot better.

This was in the first section of the letter, and he repeated the denial of torture several times. The second section was in a different pen and was different in tone as well. It was long and rambling, disjointed and vague. It was all about how he'd appreciated everything we'd tried to do for him, but he wanted us to stop now. He'd accepted his guilt and made his peace with God and was ready for justice. Let me die with dignity; there's no dignity in fighting for what's wrong instead of what's right. Once sentenced he'd lived in a state of permanent fear for several weeks, and every time they'd come 'round to wake him or feed him or take him to the exercise yard, he'd terrified himself into thinking he was about to be executed. But you can't live long with this kind of fear, he wrote. Either you go mad or you kill yourself or you lose the fear. He'd lost the fear and discovered the freedom of his tiny cell.

I spent a long time copying it all out. It was wordy, occasionally narcissistic and self-pitying, but then at times the words hit me in the gut as if they were personal messages to me. After I'd finished writing, then reading and rereading what I'd written, I sat there for quite a while not doing anything, just thinking. It was this devastating immobility of thought that had crippled me ever since the bedsit. At times it felt like a torture I couldn't escape. But there was this suspicion or fear that it might eventually lead me to a place of terrible clarity.

Everything was confused emotion and contradiction. For example, after the shock of receiving the letter had abated a little, I was overwhelmed with an intense hatred for Jarawa—as if what he'd written was one enormous rebuff of everything I'd been trying to do for him. But then moments later a warm empathy washed through me. The letter had in fact released me from the grip of some strange jealousy, an envy of all the others who'd met and knew him. Now he'd "appeared" to me as well. Unless, of course, the letter was a scam, a forgery, some sophisticated means of trying to get us to drop the campaign. But I didn't want to believe that. I couldn't believe that. Because the nearer it got to the date of his execution, the more alive he seemed to me. Perhaps he would only seem totally alive when he was dead. It was a weird thought and a disturbing one. I turned it 'round in my head but it didn't seem to mean anything.

Jamie came into my office. I hadn't spoken to him for a week or so. He didn't knock or anything; he just barged straight in as he always does. Once, a month or two back, Charlotte Fisher had come 'round to my office to pick me up for lunch and we'd started kissing and embracing and she'd even started unbuttoning her shirt and Jamie had barged in just like that, without noticing anything.

This time he was looking gleeful, smiling radiantly and rubbing his hands. "Fantastic news! Listen to this!"

He paused for effect. Had they released Jarawa perhaps? With Jarawa free, would there be anything left for me to do? I knew that it would mean the end for me, but what kind of end I couldn't yet tell. In fact it almost didn't interest me.

"Remember I told you about my niece? How I was going to send her over to do volunteer work for Freedom Africa? Remember? Hello . . . are you with me?"

"Yeah. Yes I remember."

It was something that was happening more and more frequently: someone would be talking to me, but I'd just switch off and start nodding. I'd be somewhere else. I forced my mind back to what Jamie was talking about. I remembered the conversation I'd had with him awhile back, about how he was going to send his niece to Freedom Africa to "spy" on them for us. It seemed so long ago. It was before the bedsit. Everything before the bedsit seemed such a long time ago.

"Well they fucked up," Jamie gloated. "They fucked up big time and now they've passed on the Jarawa case. That means the field's clear for us again."

He started explaining how Freedom Africa had paid for Jarawa's wife to come to the U.K., how they'd set up this unit of specialists and Oxford academics to negotiate Jarawa's release, how they'd been hoping for a big publicity coup, but the whole thing had fallen through when one of the academics involved had mysteriously disappeared. I was trying to listen, but once again my attention was sliding. I just couldn't stop it. This time it was Marianne's shaved head. I wondered why she'd done that. I wondered whether it was to make herself less sexually attractive to me, to try to repulse me. Then again, maybe it was nothing to do with me. Perhaps it was more like an act of self-mutilation. It was always in the back of my mind; it never left me. Her and the pills she took.

"Anyway the upshot is they've closed their Jarawa unit," Jamie was crowing. "The whole thing must have cost them a fortune! Now we've got to take up the slack. We've got to get in touch with Jarawa's wife and get her on board. For Christ's sake, why didn't you tell me she was in the U.K.? Have you seen her? Have you spoken to her?"

I stared down at Jamie's shoes. They were exactly the same tan color as the shoes Marianne's lover had been wearing, the ones he'd put on just before I'd killed him. It was one of those inconsequential details you remember for some reason.

"No. No, I haven't spoken to her."

"Well see if you can get a contact number. Better still, I'll get my niece to get the number from Freedom Africa."

"No Jamie. I don't know if that's the right approach."

Jamie was scowling at me. He started giving me the old spiel about how there wasn't enough money around for both us and Freedom Africa, how now was the moment to deal them the death blow. Then I explained to him about the clipping I'd received from South Africa, the article about Jarawa's wife. I said I didn't think it would be helpful to give her any public role since it was likely to blow up in our faces. I said the last thing we needed now was for anything else unsavory to emerge about Jarawa.

He started stroking his double chin. "Maybe you're right, maybe you're right. Well, of course, you must act as you see fit."

Then he hunched his shoulders and leaned closer to me. "Listen, I'll let you into a little secret. Thing is, I don't know how much longer I'll be around here."

He was in negotiations with some American software billionaire who wanted to set up an African development agency. "It's the new philanthropy—before it was art galleries, now it's human rights. They want us to think they're the good guys."

Jamie was lobbying for the position of director of this new agency. If he could swing it, he said, it could work out very well for both of us. Of course, I could end up with his present job, but what he really meant was that he'd be looking out for people for his own team. "It's worth thinking about. It'd be based in New York and there'd be serious money on the table."

I said I'd keep it in mind. For a moment the idea of going to work in New York with a big salary ignited me but then the feeling dropped away and I was left empty again. It was as though a door had opened briefly before me then slammed shut in my face. I could see Jamie glancing in the direction of my desk, with Jarawa's letter and my transcription scattered all over it. Instinctively I put my hands over the pages—I knew immediately that I was never going to show what Jarawa had written to anyone or ever tell anyone about it.

Eventually Jamie looked away then got up. "Well, anyway. Keep me informed. But you can see now how important this campaign could be for us. It could be our calling card."

He was at the door then turned back to me. "Oh by the way—I heard you on the radio last week. Very good. I don't know why you don't do more of this stuff. Jo always comes across as too touchy. I liked the torture angle. It was strong stuff."

I worked all morning, but I couldn't get Jarawa's letter out of my mind. I read it through several times. Certain strange phrases had already lodged in my mind, despite their clumsiness, despite the fact that I didn't even understand them. I remembered something Marianne had said to me once. When she was a child she'd been sent to Bible class. But she'd never really understood why Jesus had to die. Or why he'd been resurrected. In fact, she still didn't understand it. The odd thing was that it didn't interfere with her faith at all.

Around three I decided I had to get out. For an hour or so I just walked around the streets. It was hot and sticky and I could feel my buttocks slipping against each other. I hated this heat that I could take no pleasure from and longed for colder weather. I remembered how when I was a child my bedroom window would cloud up with condensation in winter and I'd draw pictures on the pane. These childhood memories that had continued to assault me since the bedsit brought on a feeling of aching sadness but I couldn't think why. My shirt was soaked from perspiration. I had a T-shirt on underneath and at one point I unbuttoned my shirt and took it off. For a while I had it tied to my waist, but in the end I dumped it in a rubbish bin.

It was an expensive shirt I'd bought in St.-Germain last time Marianne and I had been over to Paris. After dumping the shirt in the bin I could feel a wave of liberation washing through me. It was similar to what I'd felt after giving that beggar sixty pounds. But the feeling didn't last long. It was a delusion.

I'd been walking aimlessly around Bloomsbury for some time, but then I passed by an art bookshop. There was a print in the window, a medieval painting of a crucified Christ with a luminous golden background. I recognized the picture. The original was in the National Gallery, hanging right next to another painting of the same period, of a massacre scene, with bits of bodies strewn all over the canvas. I knew these paintings because sometimes we used to go to the National Gallery on school excursions. More often than not we'd bunk off to smoke dope down by the river, but I'd obviously been often enough to recognize the print in the bookshop window.

All of a sudden I was really anxious to get to the National Gallery and see those paintings again. It was odd because at school they hadn't interested me at all—except maybe that one of the massacre. What I'd liked was that it was a scene of action and yet it never changed. It was always exactly the same whenever you went to see it. The guy with the helmet was always just about to lop off the head of the guy in stockings. But he never did. The victim's face was forever frozen in terror, always a split second away from being killed and yet never killed. It was strange. Because in the end what changed was not the picture but the person looking at it. Each time you saw it you'd be older. Each time you'd be a little happier or sadder. In some way you'd be different and that was what had interested me.

I started walking fast, back in the direction of the gallery. I wanted to see all those crucified Christs again. I was thinking about them and visualizing them and their vacant, mysterious

faces, but then I started thinking about the bedsit. It came back
to me at odd moments, like flashbacks . . . the glass fragments
turning slowly in the air and glinting in the sun and the man
beckoning me, whispering to me, smiling at me . . . the beautiful
pink tulips scattered over the tiles, petals that bulged out from
the base, curved like a woman's hips. I seemed to be hovering
over the scene looking at it from the height of the ceiling or
perhaps beyond. But there was something disturbingly thought-
out and aesthetic about it all, as if it too were a painting.

I was seeing all that in my mind and then I found myself in
Trafalgar Square, drenched in sweat and breathing heavily. I
stood outside the gallery for a moment to get my breath back.
They'd built that new wing to the National; I'd completely forgotten about that. How could I have forgotten when I drove past
it every day? Perhaps they'd changed the inside of the gallery as
well. Perhaps the crucified Christ I'd seen in the bookshop window was no longer hung next to the massacre scene. It would
spoil everything for some reason. I started to go up the stairs but
then stopped and turned around again. I'd changed my mind. I'd
got myself all excited and worked up about going to the gallery
but then as soon I was outside it, the desire dropped away.

I was in my car again, driving. I drove past a police station.
Almost out of boredom, I thought of stopping and giving myself
up. But it didn't feel right, not yet. I had this idea that I would
know when the moment would be right, but perhaps that was
totally spurious. Perhaps that moment would never come. As if I
were waiting desperately for something to happen, but I didn't
even know what—some kind of release that would allow me to
move up and out of the abyss or perhaps deeper into it. Maybe
instead I would be stuck forever in this intolerable moment, like
the terrified man in the massacre painting.

It was the Jarawa case. I couldn't give myself up until that had
been resolved. Because that *had* to be resolved, one way or the

other. I mean, he'd either be executed or he wouldn't be. There was nothing indefinite about that, no halfway possibilities. In some bizarre way I even envied Jarawa for that certainty. I had the impression that if by magic I could change places with him, I would gladly do so.

Jarawa himself seemed to have given up the will to live. Even his own wife talked of him in the past tense. Perhaps there was only the slimmest chance of his survival, but for him to try to sabotage even that seemed a miserable thing. If I couldn't save Jarawa from death then I might as well be dead myself. It would be easy. I could just accelerate into that wall over there. The problem was that it would be *too* easy. Nor would it end anything. Everything that had been set in train would continue, would culminate in other events that would culminate in other events. In other words, life would go on. The only difference would be that *I* wouldn't be there. If I died now, I would be dying in utter ignorance. It was that ignorance that was impossible.

I parked the car outside the house. I hadn't even noticed I'd been driving in the direction of home. I hadn't even noticed I'd been driving at all in fact. It was this sense that the outside world was slowly disappearing under the weight of my inner world until I couldn't be sure anymore where I stopped and the rest began. I got out of the car. I could hear voices, familiar female voices but ones that didn't go together. I could hear music too. It was Marianne's favorite, that Mozart piece. It made me feel peculiar to hear that music again. I remembered lifting up the vase in the bedsit, holding it high above my head like a trophy I'd won, for one brief second.

They were all in the garden drinking white wine. Jessica was sitting on Charlotte's lap and Marianne was lying on the grass. It was a big shock to see Charlotte in my house, but it seemed almost as startling to see Marianne there with her shaved head. I still hadn't got used to it; I hadn't yet incorporated that fact into my mental image of her. I could see a little nick on the back of her neck where she'd cut herself shaving it. Jessica looked up at me uncertainly and clutched at Charlotte's shoulder. Hello, Daddy, she whispered fearfully. Marianne opened her eyes, then propped herself up on her elbows. Her eyes had that unfocused, glassy look that meant she was completely drunk. "Oh hello, darling, you're home already. Darling, I'd like you to meet Charlotte."

Charlotte put Jessica down, stood up, proffered her hand and smiled at me. "I don't believe we've met."

"No, I don't believe we have."

"Charlotte Fisher. I represent young artists, and—"

Marianne broke in. "Darling, she wants to manage me. She says she can make me squillions of pounds, darling. Darling, what do you think?"

"I don't know. That's your decision."

"That's awfully sporting of you, darling. It's all my decision then. Can I pour you some wine, darling?"

"No, thanks."

She turned to Charlotte. "He doesn't drink wine until dinner. He's awfully strict. He's awfully virtuous about everything. Puts me to shame. Spends his days saving people's lives. Don't you, darling?"

I didn't say anything. Charlotte had sat down again and Jessica had climbed back into her lap and put her hands 'round Charlotte's neck. I could feel myself shaking ever so slightly. Seeing Charlotte and Jessica together like that provoked me so much more than Marianne's mocking rants.

"Tell Charlotte about that man in Africa, darling, go on. This man they're going to execute. Go on. Well my darling's going to save the man's life. Like a superhero. Aren't you, darling?"

"Marianne. Cut it out would you please."

She looked up at me with mad eyes, a blue vein on her neck standing out horribly. For a second I thought she was going to unleash some terrible rage on me but the moment seemed to pass. She smiled. "He's so modest . . . where did you get that lighter, darling?"

I'd got out my cigarettes and I was lighting one with her lover's lighter, the one I'd taken from the bedsit. Marianne was looking at it with great curiosity.

"You gave it to me. Don't you remember?"

"Of course. Could you pass it here for a second, darling?"

I passed it to her. But she didn't light a cigarette with it. She just examined it carefully then passed it back to me wordlessly. I said, "Well . . . if you'll excuse me."

I went back into the house. On my way through I turned off the music. It wasn't disturbing me as much as it might, but I didn't want to hear it anyway. I went into the bedroom then through to the bathroom. I stood under the shower for a long time. The bedroom and bathroom doors were open and I could hear Marianne saying good-bye to Charlotte and Charlotte replying, "I want you to think about it. I understand that you feel loyal to Joseph Kimberly, but if you want me to be honest, I don't think he's really pushing your work. I just feel you deserve more."

I got out of the shower, pulled on jeans and a T-shirt, and went into the hall. Marianne closed the door on Charlotte and then walked right past me as if I wasn't there. I followed her and stopped her in the kitchen. "Listen to me. I don't want you to have anything to do with that woman. I don't like her."

Marianne spat out, "What's it to you? Who the fuck are you to tell me what to do? Who the fuck do you think you are, ordering me around?"

The vitriol of her response shocked me and all I could do was repeat lamely, "I don't want you having anything to do with her."

She wasn't listening to me anymore though. She was getting a bottle out of a crate of bottom-of-the-range Bulgarian wine that was sitting by the kitchen door. She must have ordered it in from somewhere. It was unusual, because like a lot of French people Marianne doesn't like to drink anything that isn't French.

I went back into the hall and out the front door. I could see Charlotte on the opposite side of the road, sitting in her car, revving up the engine. I ran across the road. "Hey, I want to talk to you," I shouted. The engine was running and I could see her peering up at me through the car door window—she was hesitating as to whether she should wind down the window or not. Finally she wound it down just enough so that we could hear each other. "What do you want?"

"I want to talk to you."

"Okay. You're talking to me."

"Can we go somewhere? I can't talk to you here in the middle of the road."

She shook her head. "I'm not going anywhere with you."

I'd hardly given Charlotte a passing thought since that last time I'd seen her and for a second or two my anger fell away. I thought about our liaison and the brief moments we'd been together. What struck me most was that, unlike Marianne's affair, ours had essentially been a game. Perhaps there had even been a kind of innocence in our duplicity.

"Okay then. So can you tell me what the hell you were doing in my house?"

"I think you heard Marianne. I want to represent her. I like her work. She's a rising star. I think she's being poorly managed."

"I see. And the fact that you and I slept together has got nothing to do with anything."

"Why should it? This is business."

"Business. Jesus Christ."

She exhaled sharply, almost like she was spitting something

out. "Yeah, business. Is that a scary word for you human rights people?"

I concentrated on trying to control my breathing. "You're not going to represent Marianne. Because I won't let you. I'm not having you coming 'round to my house every five minutes."

"Well it's not up to you. It's up to Marianne. And judging from what she said about you . . ."

I shook my head. "I don't care what she said about me." Then I started shouting, "I mean, what's your game, coming 'round to my house like that? What do you want? What are you trying to do to me? What did you say to her? Did you sleep with me just so you could meet her?"

She laughed uncertainly. "Yeah, right. Like I'm the scheming bitch or whatever. That's the saddest, stupidest accusation I ever heard. You're just one of these sad guys who think all women are out to get them, aren't you?"

"No. That's not true."

Suddenly I was all deflated again. Suddenly I didn't want to talk to Charlotte at all. I walked away as she accelerated into the distance. I didn't give a damn what she got up to with Marianne. What did it matter? I wouldn't be there anyway. I wouldn't be in that house; I wouldn't be with Marianne. God knows where I would be.

XIV

I'D GOT TO WORK FAIRLY EARLY, AROUND EIGHT-THIRTY, BUT FIONA told me two police officers were already waiting for me. I went into my office and flicked through the morning paper. Jarawa was on the front page for the first time in awhile. It wasn't surprising; the execution was scheduled for tomorrow. There was this weird atmosphere in the office that seemed to affect anyone who'd had anything to do with the Jarawa campaign. It was like an end and a beginning at the same time. We were gearing up for tomorrow while at the same time winding down operations. I stared out the window for a few minutes then got Fiona to show the policemen through.

They were the same ones who'd visited the house the other week—the tall, stooping, gentle-looking one who did all the talking and the short, bulky-looking one who took the notes.

They didn't seem embarrassed at all; they were obviously used to this kind of thing. I too felt calm, but then I noticed I'd been scratching one of my knuckles, almost to the point of drawing blood. As soon as I noticed it, it started to hurt and I stopped. I asked them if they'd like coffee and the tall one said yes. I got Fiona to bring it in, not because I wanted to look like I had a secretary who made me coffee, but because I was afraid my shaking would start up again. I was afraid I wouldn't be able to carry the cup without spilling it.

The tall one said, we've got some more photos of the missing man and we'd just like you to take another look, in case it triggers anything. Okay, I said. I didn't ask why they were showing them to me and not Marianne, I didn't ask why they'd come 'round to see me. The short guy passed me five or six photos. A few of them were of the man by himself, one of them was of him with another woman, who looked like she might be his wife, and then there was the last one, a blurred photo of him looking unposed and uncertain, in the countryside somewhere with a young woman who'd turned her head away so you couldn't see her face, as if at the last moment she'd decided she didn't want her picture taken after all. To anyone else it would have been unclear who it was, but I recognized it immediately as Marianne. I recognized the color of her hair and the skirt she was wearing. It was the same skirt that had been hanging over the back of the chair that day at the bedsit, although I hadn't seen her wear it since then.

I glanced through the photos, paying particular attention to the one with Marianne in it. I didn't care anymore if the police noticed. I was past that. What struck me was the comparison with that first photo of the man they'd shown us the other week. Both were blurred, but in that first one the man had been a ghostly presence; here, on the other hand, he looked very much alive.

Because it wasn't a portrait, it was like a movement that had been captured. It was also the tension between his uncertain expression and the woman with her back to the camera, as if it hid a story that you wanted to know about. How was it that this man was now dead, I wondered, when he looked so terribly alive?

Anything you recognize there, asked the policeman. I shook my head. For example, he continued, that one you're looking at now, with the woman turned away from the camera. Nothing you recognize there? Could the woman be anyone you know? I shook my head again. Impossible to say.

I straightened up the photos like a deck of cards and handed them back. The short guy was taking notes; the tall one was engaging me steadily with his eyes even as he sipped his coffee. What color was your partner's hair before she shaved it off, he asked. And did I have any ideas as to how she might have known the man? Had I discussed him with her at all? Again I shook my head. Not really, no. We didn't talk about it. I suppose it must have been like she said. I suppose he must have been a collector or something.

The policeman paused for a while, ostensibly to sip his coffee again. It was a technique to get me to fill the void out of embarrassment. I'd used that same technique myself, when I'd covered the Truth and Reconciliation Commission and had interviewed South Africans accused of atrocities. I refused the bait, but in the silence my replies hung limply in the air, their inadequacies quite apparent. For example, it was unbelievable that I hadn't spoken to Marianne about the man. If the police come 'round unannounced to your house in the evening and question your partner about some unknown man who's disappeared, it's pretty unimaginable that you wouldn't ask your partner about it once they'd gone. I wondered too why I didn't confess now and I think I must have been pretty close this time, but I could still come up with a dozen reasons why I shouldn't. I didn't want to be arrested in my own office, and also there was the fact that the Jarawa case was so close to resolution. But ultimately I knew it wasn't even that that was holding me back. It was a completely new fear, and the fear of confessing felt like the loneliness of the end. It was the terrible final ordeal I had to confront if only I had the strength.

The policeman started asking questions again. How long had Marianne and I been together, how long had we been living in the house in Camberwell, did Marianne or I own or rent any other property in London, etc. And if necessary, would I be able to account for my whereabouts on certain days last month? I answered the questions mechanically. Finally the tall one smiled at me and said well, now I think that's about everything. But we may have to speak to you again, so could I ask you if you have any plans to leave London or leave the country in the next few days? I replied no. The policeman gave me a card and said that if I changed my plans could I please give him a ring. Then as they were leaving, he said: Oh yes, just one other thing. What shoe size are you?

After they'd gone, I asked Fiona not to put any calls through to me. I just sat in my office, sweating, exhausted, staring out the window for maybe an hour or so, plagued by a steady stream of inconsequential thoughts. It occurred to me that I'd never told the police where I worked, so how did they know? Perhaps they'd phoned Marianne and she'd told them. Only Marianne wouldn't have answered the phone at eight o'clock in the morning. In fact, she never answered the phone at all anymore. Every day the tape in the answering machine was crammed with important people asking why she hadn't returned their calls. It was strange how her career was finally taking off just as everything else was collapsing.

I wished I could concentrate on other things, but it was impossible; it was all light-headedness and a vacant feeling. But then after awhile I could feel a certain relief as well. There was that new fear, but at least the doubt was gone forever. The situation was quite different from that time when I'd been picked up for going through a red light, because now there could be no more question of what the police were doing. In a weird way it was almost as if they were my protectors, leading me forward when I didn't know where to go and didn't have the courage to go there.

I was still sitting there, just staring through the window out onto the dirty brick façade of the strip club opposite when Jo came in, looking pale and worried. "Have you heard about Christian?"

"No. What about him?"

"I don't know. It's all very strange. He's just rung from a police station in Oxford. Apparently he's been detained for some reason. He wants Raoul or someone else from the legal department to go down and represent him. You haven't seen Raoul anywhere, have you?"

"No. No, I haven't."

"Okay, well . . ." She was just about to leave but then stopped and said, "Listen. You don't know anything about this do you? This business with Christian? It's got nothing to do with you?"

"I . . . No, it's got nothing to do with me. I don't know anything about it. Why should I?"

She was looking at me strangely. "I don't really know. I just thought . . . Well anyway, it doesn't matter. I'm going to try and track Raoul down then I'll probably go down to Oxford with him. Do you want to come down too?"

"Well, I don't know. Do you think there's any need for me to come?"

"No. I suppose not."

I spent a couple of hours arranging my papers and putting all the Jarawa stuff in order, writing out all the important phone

numbers and information for Jo so it would all be straightfor-
ward for her when I was gone. Because somehow I knew that
one way or another, once I left the office I'd never be back. It
gave me something to do and it was astonishing how intensely I
could plunge back into the work once I'd got started. Then at
one stage Jamie dropped by to ask me how things were going. I
said okay. I said there wasn't a lot more to do now except wait.

Jamie said, "Well, whatever happens tomorrow I think we
can call the campaign a success. We've managed to lift our profile
and that's down to you, that's thanks to your hard work."

I didn't say anything.

By eleven I was all through and I went out. It was baking
hot. I didn't know where I was going or what I was doing. There
were times when I felt calm, other times when I felt dizzy, as
though I were somewhere very high up. I passed by a church. I
didn't have a religious bone in my body, but Marianne had been
brought up a Catholic and I knew from reading her diaries that
she'd been to confession recently. I wondered what she'd confessed. I'd been so terribly ill-prepared for my own burden of
guilt and a momentary rage flared up in me. How much more
fortunate were people like Marianne, the Catholics, who could
go to confession and say a few Hail Marys. The trouble was not
even that I could never bring myself to believe in those things,
but that I was excluded in some far more fundamental way.

I kept looking over my shoulder. I couldn't believe that the
police would have just let me go like that without tailing me or
something, when they'd gone so far as to pull Christian in.
They'd pulled Christian in, I'd forgotten that. The trouble was
that there were too many things to remember. Too much to take
in, like I was just endlessly sucking in all these events and expe-
riences deep into the nowhere of myself. They'd got Christian
and Jo was on her way to see him. What a shame he hadn't made

it to West Africa first as he'd planned; it was my fault. No doubt they'd traced my call to Christian from the bedsit. It was simple, so simple that it was remarkable it hadn't occurred to me before.

The more I thought about Christian, the more I wondered why he did what he did and why he'd helped me, the more mystified I was by his action. I wondered if it was guilt. I wondered if he'd fantasized about killing his wife or something, when suddenly she'd died in the accident, taking it out of his hands. I wondered if that was the thing he'd wanted to tell me. But it was pure speculation: the idea had only occurred to me because I wanted it to be true. Finally the only real answer I could come up with was that he'd helped me simply because I'd asked him to. Whereas I had called Christian for the opposite reason—to share in my misfortune. The shame was there just below the surface, welling up under my eyes like pus under a bruise, ready to break out any moment at the slightest pressure, for anything or for nothing. I was crossing the road and somehow I was quite certain I'd never make it to the other side. I was sure a car would come hurtling out of nowhere to knock me down and I closed my eyes and whispered: "Help me now. Please help me now." I was talking to Jarawa or praying to him and I could see his face before me.

The next thing I knew I was lying on the footpath. Some guy was there, standing over me, helping me up, saying you all right, mate? Yeah, I replied, just slipped, that's all. I'd passed out, for a second or two only, but I'd passed out nonetheless. It was the first time anything like that had happened to me. I sat down on a bench by a bus stop. I should have been feeling groggy, but I wasn't at all. In fact I was feeling better, really much better, as if my head had somehow been cleared of everything that had been tormenting me.

• • •

Jessica was sitting on the kitchen floor, whispering to herself, playing some game that involved slow, repetitive movements, like those of a caged animal in a zoo. There was no creativity to her movements; in fact, it was the very reverse of play and I could immediately see that something wasn't right with her. "What's up, Jess?"

At first she appeared to be deep in concentration and acted as if she hadn't heard or noticed me, but then eventually she said in a tiny voice, "Maman's sick."

"Why, what's wrong with her?"

"Maman's sick."

She wouldn't say anything else, though. For once I controlled myself and didn't berate her as a feeling of dread spread through me. I ran out the back door, across the garden, and into the studio. . . . She'd stuck the bed right in the middle of the room for some reason, like it was a stage or place of execution. And she was lying there like a Victorian consumptive in her nightgown, stained red, staring at me glassily. I ripped off her nightgown and ran my hands over her body, looking for the wound, but it wasn't that. It wasn't what I'd thought. What it was, was that she was hemorrhaging. Or had been hemorrhaging. It was impossible to tell whether it had stopped or not, but her face and body looked almost like marble and she was limp and wasn't speaking at all. She was just staring vacantly.

I got my dressing gown from the bedroom and wrapped it 'round her then I heaved her off the bed and into my arms. It wasn't so easy though. She'd put on quite a bit of weight recently, maybe it was being pregnant or maybe it was the drinking. I hadn't had her in my arms like that in such a long time and I hadn't felt her skin for weeks. As I crossed back over the garden with her I noticed that her lips were moving. I couldn't hear anything, but I could lip-read easily enough. What she was trying to say was "Look after Jessica."

I said, "What do you mean? Of course I'm looking after Jessica. We're both looking after Jessica. Jessica's fine."

Jessica was still on the kitchen floor, playing her repetitive game. I carefully laid Marianne down on the sofa and got a sponge from the bathroom to clean off the worst of the blood, but it wasn't easy. It was everywhere. How had she got it even on her forehead and the stubble of her head, as if it were for some macabre ritual?

"Now listen, Jess. It was really good you told me about Mummy because she's not well at all and we're going to have to go to the hospital now. What I need you to do is go ahead of me and open the doors and then the car door while I carry Mummy. Okay?"

Jessica obeyed wordlessly. I heaved Marianne up again and carried her through the house and out the front door then laid her on the backseat of the car. But she didn't look comfortable at all so I got a pillow from the bedroom to rest her head on, and a blanket as well. Then I suddenly remembered something I'd seen or read, about people who'd lost blood and how they should be given liquids and I ran into the kitchen and filled up an old wine bottle with tap water and took it back to the car.

"Okay? Comfortable? Why don't you drink this? It's only water."

She wouldn't though. She was still looking at me in that glassy way and then she beckoned me feebly with her hand, exactly the same gesture as her lover's, that way he'd beckoned me just before he'd died. It was a shock and I leaned close to Marianne's face and wiped some of the spit from her mouth. She was trying to say "Look after Jessica" again.

"Of course I'll look after Jessica! We'll both look after Jessica! Nothing's going to happen to Jessica! Why are you being so damned melodramatic about everything?"

I tried to laugh for encouragement, but it came out all strangulated. I stuck Jessica in beside me and readjusted the rearview mirror so that I could keep an eye on Marianne lying on the backseat. She kept on moving her lips. It was this thing about Jessica. Jessica herself just sat there, silently, looking straight ahead like a zombie. Then as we were driving I couldn't stop myself repeating: "Of course I'll look after Jessica! Of course I will! We both will!" In a way I believed it too and I wanted to believe it, while at the same time there was that other thing, which was the blackness and the guilt. I wasn't going to be here of course. I wasn't going to look after Jessica at all. She said: I'm tired Daddy, and laid her head down on my thigh.

I was heading for St. Stephen's, where my friend Alex worked in casualty, but whether he'd be there today I didn't know. I kept looking at Marianne in the rearview mirror. At first I thought she'd be okay, for a very stupid reason. It was because I'd managed to understand what she'd been saying to me when she'd beckoned me, unlike at the bedsit. It was a kind of super-stition, but I really believed it. Then just as we got to the hospital she started shaking in this unnatural way. I stopped the car outside the casualty entrance and shouted out to an ambulance guy or porter or whatever and we carried her through. We took her straight through to the emergency unit and she was still shaking like she was having a seizure. They transferred her to a bed then this young male doctor started firing a string of ques-tions at me: how old was Marianne, what were her symptoms etc. I told him about Marianne being pregnant and hemorrhag-ing and how I also suspected that she'd taken sleeping tablets, maybe mixed with alcohol. As I was saying all this and answering the doctor's questions another emergency was beginning to unfold on the other side of the ward. They'd rushed in this young guy who'd been in a car accident. He was being very dif-ficult to manage. He kept shaking off the two nurses who were trying to get his clothes off and get him to lie down. He kept on sitting up and saying, "Listen, I'm not staying here. I feel fine, there's nothing wrong with me!" Then he looked in my direction for a split second and smiled insanely and I could see this ghastly open wound on the side of his head.

A nurse hustled me out of the emergency unit and into a waiting room. I asked her if Alex was on duty and she said she'd go and check for me and then she left. Everything had happened so quickly, as if in a blur of words and images, and it was difficult to collect my thoughts.

I lit a cigarette. The nurse came back, she said Alex would be down shortly. She frowned and said that smoking wasn't permitted anywhere in the hospital.

"For God's sake. I've just brought my wife in. For God's sake . . ."

My hands were trembling as I spoke. The nurse shook her head with simulated compassion, "I'm really sorry, but I'm afraid smoking's not allowed here."

"Well, I'm going to smoke anyway."

She looked surprised and pissed off but she didn't say anything and just walked out again. The only other person in the waiting room was a tramp with his left hand all wrapped in a bandage, which he waved in my direction. Got a cigarette, he said. I gave him one. If I'd told her what you just told her they'd have chucked me out, he said.

Suddenly I remembered Jessica. In all the panic I'd forgotten about her and couldn't remember where she'd been, whether she'd got out of the car or not. I got up and strode back through the emergency unit to the entrance. I couldn't see Marianne anywhere. They must have moved her to another ward or something.

There were a couple of guys in uniforms standing by the car, one was talking into a walkie-talkie. It's my car, I said. Well, you'll have to move it, mate, he replied. I opened the door. Jessica was lying on the floor, curled up in fetal position, sucking her thumb and shivering. In the shadows I could see the profile of her nose, already so much like Marianne's. I picked her up. What were you doing down there, I asked, but she didn't say anything; she was shivering.

I moved the car to the car park then walked back to the waiting room with Jessica in my arms. The tramp was still there. He started talking, but I wasn't paying attention, I was watching Jessica. She'd been dozing, but now she'd woken up. She struggled out of my arms and sat down beside me and rubbed her eyes with the exaggerated gestures of a child. She sat there staring into space for a while but then eventually turned to me and said, "Daddy, when will I have to go to school?"

"Not for a long time, Jessica. Not for over a year."

"I don't want to go to school."

"Everyone has to go to school."

"I don't want to. I'm not going to school."

"Not ever?"

"Not ever."

"Well, perhaps you're right. I don't know."

We both fell silent. It was hard to concentrate on any one thing. I lit another cigarette with the Zippo, then gave one to the tramp. He was half talking to me, half talking to himself. "They're happy to fix up my hand then sling me out, see. If I got some rare disease they'd spend thousands of pounds fixing me up then sling me out, see."

Alex came in. He looked quite different in a white coat, more the authority figure and less the friend. I could see he was just about to launch into all that crap about how we hadn't seen each other in ages and I jumped up from my seat to preempt him. "How is she, is she okay?"

"Well, she's not in any danger," he said, looking vaguely taken aback by my abruptness. They'd put her on a drip and pumped her stomach for good measure and they were going to keep her in hospital under observation for twenty-four hours. Of course, he continued, you've probably already guessed the bad news. I nodded, but then shook my head. She never wanted it, I blurted out despite myself, in a way that's what it's all about, she was doing her best to get rid of it. Alex looked incredibly uncomfortable, but it didn't bother me. It didn't bother me anymore to say such things to him or to anyone else. It bothered me to say it in front of Jessica though, despite the fact that she couldn't even understand.

"The thing is to get her to see someone," Alex was saying. He'd been talking all this time, but I hadn't been listening. "What do you mean," I replied, "get her to see someone?" "Well, like a psychiatrist, for example," he continued.

"Psychiatrist? A psychiatrist? A psychiatrist is the last person she needs to see!"

"Okay. Now calm down, calm down . . ."

I'd been getting all heated up and was almost shouting. Jessica was there standing beside me, holding my hand, tugging at it.

Alex said, "Listen, are you all right?"

"What do you mean?"

I stared at him like he was a stranger. He was one of those people you continue to see because you went to school with them or whatever but what did I really know of him? What did I know of anyone?

"Are you going to be okay driving? I mean, I know this has been really traumatic and everything."

"Yeah. I'll be fine. Thanks. No I mean it, thanks for everything."

It was these terrible swings, one moment despising someone and the next tearfully grateful. He started going on about how we hadn't seen each other for ages and how we should all get together sometime, me, Marianne, Alex and Suzie. That would be great, I replied mechanically.

"Listen, I've just had this brilliant idea. We've got these tickets to see a play by that woman Marianne was going on about last time we came to your place, Sarah something. I think it's the weekend after next. Why don't you and Marianne come along too and then we could have dinner afterward? That is, if Marianne's well enough by then."

"Yeah. That'd be great."

There was an uncomfortable pause. Alex's suggestion hung in the air as if it were something distasteful, like an obscene joke at a funeral. The idea of seeing a play the weekend after next seemed like a dream. The idea of doing anything at all in a fortnight's time seemed quite unimaginable.

Once we'd got back from the hospital I woke Jessica up and put her in a chair by the kitchen table and started preparing her dinner. She'd been dozing in my arms, but I knew what she was like. I knew if I didn't feed her now she'd sleep for an hour or two then wake up and turn hyperactive again. I talked to her to keep her awake. "And who's that one a picture of?"

I was looking at the drawing Marianne had pinned to the wall. But Jessica was paying no attention to me and I had to repeat the question. Finally she said, "It's the man. The man in the mask."

"What man in the mask?"

"The one I told you about. A million times."

"Which one?"

She suddenly slid off her chair, all excited, and started shouting: "It's you, silly, it's you! It's you again! I told you before!" She was giggling maniacally, like it was a tremendously funny joke.

"Okay, Jessica. Calm down now."

I got her to eat her food without too many problems, but then it took ages to get her to go to sleep. She kept asking where

Marianne was and I'd tell her she was at the hospital, but she wasn't listening. She was building up to some kind of hysterical fit and I just kept talking to her softly and patiently. Eventually she started to doze off in spite of herself, still murmuring and muttering in her sleep, and I slipped quietly out of the room. I wandered around the house at a loss as to what to do with myself, then went and sat outside in the garden. It was incredibly quiet for London and there was this ache of loneliness that pervaded and colored everything.

The door to Marianne's studio was open and it occurred to me that I'd better go and clean up inside. I went in. Everything felt strangely barren, as though some powerful force had swept through and then left forever. The bloody sheets were piled up on the bed and her ripped nightgown was lying crumpled on the floor like the aftermath of some unimaginable ritual act. There were a lot of clothes lying messily on the floor. I sifted through them, picking out a skirt, top and some underwear to take to Marianne when I went to the hospital tomorrow morning. Then under all the clothes I noticed papers and stuff as well. There was that photo of her grinning wildly, the one that had been at the bedsit. I tried to picture Marianne going back to clear out the bedsit. I tried to imagine her there, packing things into boxes, her face totally impassive, or maybe with tears in her eyes, who knows? But how was it that I hadn't thought of all these things before, how was it that I so lacked the imagination? There were pages of writing, scribbled in Marianne's characteristic mix of English and French. Most of it was illegible, but certain phrases sprang out accusingly at me. "Grieving him, angry at him for disappearing like that. But you can't be angry at the dead for long ..." Then, a little further on. "... but he was a *gentle* man!" It shook me when I read that. I knew she was writing about her lover and not me. The worthlessness of everything I'd done rose up around me as I put the pages down and walked back into the garden.

XV

IT WAS MAYBE A DREAM OF THE MAN AT THE MOUTH OF THE CAVE, hands stretched toward me and the smile I had never forgotten, but then I woke up and the memory slipped away. I got up and went through to the kitchen to put the kettle on and on the way I noticed the blinking light on the answering machine. There were the usual messages for Marianne asking where she was, and there were several for me too, from the office. Where had I disappeared to yesterday afternoon? Jo wanted to speak to me urgently. Her voice sounded strained, but she didn't say whether it was about Christian or Jarawa. Perhaps she'd found the note on my desk. Today was the twenty-second of August, after all. After the constant focus on that date it had still somehow crept up on me and caught me unawares.

I got Jessica dressed and fed then drove her to the day care center. The supervisor was clearly surprised to see her and I remembered that Jessica hadn't actually been there for some time now—she'd been spending her days with Marianne in the studio. In the car she'd been sitting beside me gripping my thigh, but once we'd got inside the building she was eager to get away and play with her friends. I squeezed her hand harder. "Don't leave me now, Jessica," I whispered to her, "don't leave me now." Of course, she didn't have the faintest clue what I was going on about, I was maybe embarrassing or even scaring her. The supervisor too was looking at me strangely. I let go of Jessica's hand and suddenly she bounded off in the direction of a little Chinese boy. I turned back toward the car to drive to the hospital.

There'd been this nervousness about seeing Marianne again. But after dropping Jessica off it was as if I'd been cleaned of all emotion, and I could face it now with equanimity. A nurse showed me into a ward of ten beds. Marianne was sitting up in her bed, staring into space, wearing a hospital gown that opened at the front. She looked a little better than I expected but no longer beautiful. There was the shaved head I'd never got used to, but now she was pale and bloated as well. Her skin was blotchy, her breasts hung heavily, and there were new lines on her face.

"I brought you some clothes—"

"Where's Jessica?"

"Don't worry. She's at the day care center."

I sat on the bed for quite a while without either of us saying anything or even looking at each other. Instead I looked 'round for the guy I'd seen yesterday with the head wound, but he wasn't there, which didn't mean anything of course. There were things I wanted to say to Marianne, but here didn't feel like the place; although who knows whether I'd get another opportunity now.

Marianne had been staring out the window opposite her bed, but her gaze suddenly switched to me. She was staring at me fiercely. "I don't want you to leave me here."

"I'm not going to leave you here. I'm not going to leave you anywhere."

"I've had enough. I want to get out."

"I thought you had to stay here until tonight."

"I don't want to. They gave me this disgusting soup. I want to get out now. I don't want you to leave me here."

I drew the curtains 'round her bed and helped her put on the clothes I'd brought her, then helped her up. She was pretty weak, but it seemed like she could walk all right. Then once we were in the corridor a nurse came running up to us. Are you leaving, she asked in astonishment, could you please wait until I get Doctor Moran. Marianne stared at her unblinkingly, blankly, leaning on me for support. She wasn't quite right in the head yet, but I knew it would pass. I knew it from her depressive fits in the past.

The skies were gradually clearing in my mind—everything felt lighter now that Marianne was here beside me in the car, essentially out of danger. The only shadow was the thought that the police would be there waiting for me at home to deny me these last moments with her. For a split second I even considered not going home at all. I had this vision of driving down to this village by the sea in Dorset where Marianne and I had once gone for a holiday, and where Jessica had probably been conceived. Then again, if I did that, who would pick up Jessica from the day care center? I looked at Marianne and realized she'd be too weak for the trip anyway. There was no way out of it.

But in the end there was no one waiting at the house. Once I'd got Marianne home, I undressed her and got her into the shower and washed her while she just stood there staring at the tiles on the wall, letting me take care of her like she was an old woman, lifting her arms when I told her to. After I'd dried her I could see the color rising to her cheeks and she definitely looked better. She said she still felt weak though and needed to lie down for a bit. It was the first time she'd lain down on our bed in awhile. As the days had gone by without her there in bed beside me the smell of her body and hair had gradually disappeared from the sheets and the room and even from my memory, but it seemed to be almost overpowering me now. She was lying on the bed with her legs up, carefully examining her thighs. Cellulite, she said, I've never noticed it before. . . . It's age, I'm getting old. I could see the glistening of her eyes. Don't worry, I said, I'm here now. But it was a strange thing for me to say and it occurred to me that the peculiarity of that phrase was that no one who said it could ever be wrong.

I let her doze for a while, an hour or so, while I sat in the kitchen with a whole stack of papers from the study. I was doing the same thing I'd done at work. I was organizing everything to make it easier for Marianne. She'd always left the financial arrangements to me—all the paperwork for the house, bank, taxes, Jessica's endowment, etc. Now I was making a list of where everything was and what she had to do and when, and who she had to contact. She would have to learn to do all that, now that I wasn't going to be around anymore.

Every few minutes the phone rang. I had the answering machine turned off, but the ringing started to get on my nerves and I pulled the jack out of the wall. It was the office or the newspapers maybe, no doubt they were calling about Jarawa and I knew he was still there behind me, that he was there in my mind as I prepared for my not being here anymore. Perhaps Jarawa was already dead. I couldn't think about it. In a way my relationship with him didn't depend on whether he was dead or alive at this exact moment. I looked up at the picture tacked to the kitchen wall, the one Jessica had drawn. I ripped it off the wall and crumpled it up into a ball and put my cigarette to it until it flamed up and I threw it into the sink.

Marianne appeared. She'd dressed and put some lipstick on, which had the effect of softening the impact of her shaved head. She looked so much better now than she had at the hospital, but I could tell she was still pretty vague. It's such a lovely day she said, let's go somewhere. She opened the kitchen door and light flooded in from the back garden. It was true, it was a hot and beautiful day, but I hadn't really noticed until Marianne had pointed it out. What a fantastic summer it had been, how blessed we'd been with warmth. . . . Are you sure you'll be all right I asked, and she nodded childishly.

Once we were in the car again Marianne said, "I know. Let's go and get Jessica. Let's have a day out, just the three of us."

They were very funny with us at the day care center and the supervisor looked strangely at Marianne with her shaved head. She kept on asking all these questions as to why we wanted to take Jessica out, as if she had some say in the matter. It made me wonder: Would Marianne have some social worker coming 'round every week to annoy her and tell her to stop drinking once I'd gone? The other kids were all watching a cartoon on television and at first Jessica didn't want to leave, but when Marianne started to get upset and tearful she seemed to change her mind. "Pick me up then."

"Daddy'll pick you up. You're too big for me now."

We were in the car again, all three of us. There seemed to be such a lot of police cars on the road, or perhaps there always were and I was only noticing it now. Every time we passed one, I started shaking again until the car was out of sight and then the shaking would subside.

"So where do you want to go Jessica? To the park? The zoo? We'll take you anywhere you want."

"The toy shop. Can you open the roof, Daddy?"

We'd just crossed the river, over Albert Bridge. I remembered that story about the man who'd tipped a total stranger into the river from Albert Bridge. Just the day before at the office I'd come across a second article about it, in the *Guardian*. It was an interview with the victim after he'd been to see his assailant in custody. What had impressed him, he'd said, was how very mild-mannered his attacker was. The man had never alluded to why he'd done it, he'd just very politely apologized and seemed incredibly relieved when his victim forgave him. And then he'd said that he would have had to kill himself if his victim hadn't forgiven him.

I parked the car off the King's Road and we walked to Peter Jones and went to the toy department. Jessica was getting all excited and started running around the place. Marianne was trying to calm her down and bent down to pick her up, but then she got all giddy and had to sit down for a while. Jessica and I left her by the till and we started going 'round the shelves to pick out some toys.

"How about this teddy bear," I said, grabbing one from the shelves. "He's a very handsome bear, don't you think?"

Jessica took the bear wordlessly.

"What are you going to call him then, Jess?"

"Dunno . . ."

I could see her attention had already been drawn by something else. It was a snow dome, with an out-of-season nativity scene. Mary, Joseph, baby Jesus, and a few animals.

"You pick it up and shake it. See?"

I'd given it a good shake then crouched down with it so Jessica could see too, and we were both staring intensely at the little figures. It was a cheap model from Taiwan; the plastic figures had been painted in a very approximate fashion without any attempt at expression. Joseph stood by impotently with his crooked staff, but in the emptiness of Mary's face I fancied I could see and understand the suffering open up to me.

"Who are they? Who are they, Daddy?"

I tore my gaze from the snow dome. "Maybe they're us."

"Are they? No they're not."

"How do you know that?"

"'Cause inside it's a baby, but I'm not a baby anymore. I'm grown up."

"You're right. I hadn't thought of that."

She was still staring at it with wide-eyed fascination. "Shake it again."

I shook it. "But if I buy it for you, you'll have to be careful with it. They're very easy to break. You couldn't drop it, for example."

"I'll be careful with it. I promise."

I paid for the teddy bear and snow dome and looked 'round for Marianne, but she'd disappeared. For a moment I panicked, but that peculiar sense of strain had left me. We hung around the toy department waiting for her and I showed Jessica how to shake the snow dome slowly with both hands so it wouldn't slip out of her grip. I saw a kid Jessica's age and his mother walking down the aisles. They were holding hands. I didn't think anything of it, but then I saw that the kid had something stuck on a finger on his free hand. It was the little banana man I'd given him at the police station, not so long ago. As they walked by, the woman gave me that vacant smile parents give each other. She hadn't recognized me. Her son had though—he stopped all of a sudden in front of me. He looked up and showed me his finger. I noticed his almond eyes and stubby hands. I saw what it was about his elfin-like face now: he had Down's syndrome. I hadn't realized before. His expression seemed preternaturally solemn. In its stillness, it was as though the child were not three or four but eighty-four.

Eventually Marianne came back, all smiles. She suddenly took out something from behind her back. "Happy Birthday!"

It was a package, wrapped like a present. I hadn't exactly forgotten that it was my birthday. Rather, everything had been subsumed by Jarawa, he'd taken over my birthday until in reality it was his day now, not mine. Still it was strange to think that I was now thirty and would never again be in my twenties. I opened the present. It was a watch. I'd never said anything to her but she'd nonetheless noticed that I'd lost my watch and she'd bought me this new one. The hands were still but then I shook it and the second hand immediately sprang to life.

We bought some food and we were going to go to the park, but then Jessica suddenly said I want to go home now. Okay, I said. I could have insisted on the park, but perhaps she was right after all. The fear of the police was still there, but it was fading fast. And all the time I was driving I was thinking of the doctor who'd pushed that man into the river. What really struck me now was the fact that he'd said he'd have killed himself if he hadn't been forgiven. It was something that only weeks ago would have been quite incomprehensible to me. I knew that if by some miracle Marianne's lover were to walk into our house now, he would have the perfect right to destroy me and I couldn't or wouldn't do anything to stop him. And yet, at the same time, I felt curiously angry with him, or was it maybe angry at myself, for letting him so definitively have the last word.

There was a slight tightening of the heart muscles as I rounded the corner of our street, but there were no police there. Jessica went outside to play in the garden with her new teddy bear and the snow dome while Marianne and I prepared lunch. But after a few moments I put my arms around her for the first time in ages and it felt good. We stayed like that for a while with Marianne's head resting on my shoulder, then eventually we disentangled ourselves and sat down wordlessly at the kitchen table.

I looked up at where Jessica's drawing had been tacked to the wall before I'd ripped it down and I could see the pin holes in the wall that marked its absence. Marianne had her elbows on the table; she was staring into the garden and seemed very far away. "There was a time when I was going to leave you."

"I know that."

"I'm not going to leave you now. Ever."

"I know that."

She was still staring through the open door to Jessica, who was sitting on the grass shaking the snow dome then shaking it again. "She's going to break it."

"No she's not. She promised me she wouldn't. It'll be all right."

Marianne was speaking slowly and unnaturally like she sometimes does after taking sleeping pills. "It's like I've been drifting through life. . . . It's the routine that destroys me. Then when the storm came I had to lash myself to the mast."

"Yes," I replied mechanically, "lashed to the mast."

The sun splashed through the door, drenching the room, draining Marianne's face of color like she was a saint in a medieval painting. It was hot, so hot, and yet the whisper of autumn was not so very far away . . . there would be relief from the heat, the first coolness in the air, the nights getting longer, darker. . . . I got up to take the lunch things through to the table in the garden and grabbed a bottle of white wine from the fridge.

After lunch we lay down on the grass together, with Marianne's head resting on my stomach. The heat was mesmerizing. I could feel it penetrating and relaxing the muscles throughout my body, and I watched Marianne's chest and stomach expand and subside slowly and regularly with her breathing. I was about to close my eyes, but then my attention was drawn to a bird, a sparrow, that was daring to come right up to us to peck at the crumbs we'd left. It was so close that I could have hit it with a swing of my arm and killed it. I watched it without moving. I could see its tiny breast palpitating so frantically, so desperately compared with the slow, solemn pulse of Marianne's heartbeat, which seemed to reverberate right through me. It was as if I were beyond anything that could harm me now, and not even death had the power to take anything away from me. I remembered the extraordinary sense of well-being that had possessed me that day in the park after identifying Susan Tedeschi's body. It had perplexed me at the time, but what it had been, I now realized, was merely an anticipation of this moment, because I was sure that I'd never felt happier than I felt now, as if I were somehow frozen in free fall and staring down at the most bewitching landscape.

Marianne was saying, "Let's get away, I mean for good. I'm sick of London, I'm sick of cities. . . . Let's sell up and buy a house near Montargues, near Papa, sooner or later he'll need someone to look after him and there's only me. . . ."

"Yes, let's do that," I replied, momentarily buried in this fantasy of moving to the south of France, deep in a memory of that stream we'd found one summer that cut through the dry rock of the Midi and the peculiar echoing sound of water on pebbles. It was a dream that fed off a suspicion, which even now was so hard to be completely rid of, that such things were still possible. I had to fight against this temptation to believe in a future: it was the poison that would ruin everything between Marianne and me. I watched Jessica shaking the snow dome, in turns curious, delighted, impatient, but never bored. The thing that impressed me was her concentration on it to the exclusion of everything else, even to the exclusion of herself. Why was it such a beautiful thing to see?

"I know," Marianne suddenly said, "let's play backgammon. We haven't played backgammon in such a long time."

It was true that we used to play it a lot in the early days

before Jessica, and often in bed after we'd made love in the mornings. I got up now and went inside to get the board. I stopped in the kitchen, still dazed by the heat. My new watch glinted in the sun, reflecting its rays and making curious patterns on the white walls. I thought of turning on the radio to listen to *The World at One*, surely they'd have the news about Jarawa by now. I couldn't bring myself to do it though. In a way, it didn't seem to matter anymore. I wondered what would happen to his cousin, his wife. A vision of Jarawa filled me, it was that old photo of him in his three-piece suit, expanding in my mind until it enveloped everything. His mouth was moving; he was telling me something; it was important. The stone had been rolled away. He was alive again. The living presence of the dead rose up around me, transfiguring the day.

I was watching Marianne from the kitchen. She was still lying on the grass. I was remembering various things about her, going right back to the beginning and those first few nights together in her flat in Menilmontant. What was it that we'd created out of thin air? What was that impossible thing we'd never talked about because we never wanted to disturb it, were afraid that it wouldn't survive such an expression? It was the memory of all the things I'd lost . . . the pleasure of drinking wine and lying on the grass . . . the pleasure of seeing Marianne naked . . .

I heard the sound of a car and I looked up through the kitchen window. It was a police car pulling up outside our house. In any case I'd already known that the moment had come; I'd felt it inside me. I almost wasn't thinking about it but then I could hear the doorbell, that annoyingly suburban ding-dong I'd been meaning to change to a buzz for so long and now never would. I went out of the kitchen and walked down the corridor—it seemed such a long way to the front door and so difficult to get there, as if somehow I were a child once again, taking my first steps. There was the mirror hanging in the corridor, but in my mind's eye it was an altogether different mirror, the one that had hung above the fireplace in the bedsit where I'd killed a man, not so long ago. I could see myself staring into it and touching it with my hand, trying to connect with this image of myself that perhaps I believed I could dissolve into. The doorbell rang again.

Now I was at the front door and I opened it. On the doorstep were the same two policemen, the tall one and the bulky one. Why had I finally waited for them to come to me rather than going to them? It was the sole thing that came to mind because the rest was calmness and surrender. The tall one seemed momentarily lost for words and I took the initiative. "Could I at least say good-bye to my wife and daughter?"

"Of course."

I noticed that the bulky one had a holster and gun, which was unusual. On the other hand, perhaps it was standard issue for policemen who were about to arrest a murderer. A crazy notion to lunge for the gun seized me, but it was a confused idea. Was it to kill myself or was it to escape? But neither of those options were of any use to me. Neither took me to a place that I would have preferred to go, anywhere better than where the police were about to lead me. Fragments of memories kept returning to me, things I'd suppressed. I remembered now how I'd woken up on the morning of the murder with a horrible sense of dread that was quite new and strange. I remembered thinking: What's wrong with me? What's got into me? I'd walked to my car with this intolerable sadness weighing down on me so that I could almost feel it as a physical burden and it took all my strength to keep moving. I remembered being down by the canal in Camden and the tears streaming down my face. Perhaps at the time I'd thought—if I'd thought at all—that they were in some way related to what I'd just gone through with Charlotte. Now I knew otherwise. They were the tears of anticipation. Tears of mourning for what I was about to do.

The policemen followed me through to the kitchen, then waited there while I continued on into the garden. Marianne was sitting up now—she could see the police easily enough through the open kitchen door. She was fiddling with her hands, fiddling with the plain silver ring I'd given her years ago and that I thought she'd lost. I sat down beside her and put my hand to her face. "I'm sorry. I'm so sorry."

"But did he suffer? Did you hurt him?"

"No. I didn't hurt him."

I kissed her on the forehead then on her dry lips. We stared at each other intensely for a while. Everything felt so very calm and peaceful. I looked over to the policemen. They didn't seem in any particular hurry and I knew that they would be kind to me. I kept looking at Jessica as well. She was talking to her new teddy bear and showing it how to hold the snow dome, just as I had shown her at the toy department. Her skin would be burning under this sun and I thought to get her hat for her and some sunscreen from the bathroom, but I knew that the moment I got up the spell would be broken and it would be over for ever. Marianne and Jessica, the garden, the birds and the leaves, everything seemed so still, frozen in this blur of heat and life like an old photograph I would never forget. The feeling of being cleansed of all hope washed through me, purifying me until I realized I was finally standing at the threshold of my own story, ready to stretch out and start again.

Acknowledgments

I HAVE ADAPTED A FEW LINES FROM THE FOLLOWING ARTICLES and authors: "At the Morgue" by Helen Garner (in *True Stories*, Text Publishing, 1996) and "Someone Take These Dreams Away" by Jon Savage (*Mojo*, July 1994).

Thanks to my family, in particular Patrick Wilcken, for his editorial input. Thanks also to Lisa Darnell, Jody Johnson, Philip Gwyn Jones, and Jon Butler.

And a special thank-you to Julie, for her love and support.